CW01237366

The second in the Elementalists series

Darkness

Copyright © 2010 by Hannah S. Chacko

Cover design by Thomas. J. M. Cook

Book design by Hannah S. Chacko

All rights reserved.

No part of this book may be reproduced in any form or by any electronic or mechanical means including information storage and retrieval systems, without permission in writing from the author. The only exception is by a reviewer, who may quote short excerpts in a review.

Anyone violating this will be tracked down by the Oathkeepers.

Published by Lulu

ISBN 978-0-557-44082-5

As ever, for Thomas J.M Cook, my life and my love. Where would I be without you? You give me strength and keep me going when I stray from writing. And from you, the Elder from Cloric came into being in order to save my books.

For the Monster Raving Loony Party for brightening many a cloudy day.

For all my friends who supported me as times got tough.

And in loving memory of Scarien Éscaronôvic, who sacrificed himself for the good of the many.

Introduction

To all readers in all realms, young and old,

You may, or may not, be aware that this is the second chapter in the lives of the *Children of Destiny*. But that is irrelevant. All new readers may be slightly confused at first, but this chapter is as good on its own as it is when following the first. Although, if you have not read the previous instalment, and do find yourselves confused at any point, the only way to resolve this is to actually read *The Lie* and familiarise yourself with the story so far. That way, you can also familiarise yourselves with the characters beginning this tale.

This latest instalment is full of its ups and downs. Many events are rather unpleasant and upsetting, whereas others are worth rejoicing over. This rather chaotic pattern is as accurate as can be, though many events have been emphasised in great detail, whilst others are skimmed over to smooth some of the story out, and to account for missing details.

Though it may still seem, to all fourth-realmers, far

away and irrelevant, I assure you, the struggle draws closer. It will not be long before these events occur much closer to home. However, as before, we pick up in Catré, and this follows on directly from what you may, or may not, have previously read.

However, more realms are quickly involved as the children begin to Travel more. Soon, 'Earth' will be drawn into this fateful struggle.

This particular chapter soon moves to Cyphia, the ninth realm and from there our protagonists, and others, must venture to a realm where mortals cannot remain without a native to keep them there. Also, the fourth-realm may be visited briefly soon, but not the fourth-realm as you readers know it.

Should you have any difficulties with the names or wish to learn a little about each character, the Information and Pronunciation Guide towards the end of the tale has once again been included. You know where to find me if you wish to learn more beyond this, if you have read the first book. If not, then I say again, email me at the_elementalists@yahoo.com for questions that cannot wait to be answered. I strive to answer all emails individually, and, at present, I am succeeding. For your own additional reading and enjoyment, you can also visit my website: www.wix.com/hschacko/home. On those pages, there is more to discover should you look in the right places.

The *Children of Destiny* will gain many unlikely friends in this chapter, and while they remain the only ones truly essential to our survival, the actions of these allies and the actions of others may seriously influence their, and our, futures. Although these books follow the *Children of Destiny*, you will find that in many places, I am writing the accounts of other characters also.

The Clorans have a very important tale to tell, and while the Zyrons for the most part are left behind, quite soon the Letrans become the vital group in the war. Other characters are finding things about themselves that can change the course of many events to come, and as a result, the tale may seem to jump around. Many events are happening at any one time and to follow each one individually for an extended period of time would cause some important details to be forgotten. Instead, with almost every chapter break, there may be a jump to another realm or place in the realms. These events will gradually be tied together and will not include more than four stories for very long.

As it stands, there are three main focuses for this

chapter in the tale and you will come to realise them as we continue. One is definite and already known: the *Children of Destiny*, although they are not as certain as they may seem. Another is the quest of the Clorans and the final one is the actions of the Vertex and the happenings on Vantrörkî; these movements will continue to shape the course of the future.

Brief updates may be found throughout the text of other places and new characters may be introduced much earlier than they are needed. This will only help to ease them into events later on.

As I have said in the previous book, these events are merely recorded as I have been told. Many of the people included in these writings are long since lost, but thanks to others who endure the ravages of time, their tales may never be forgotten.

Again, I must also stress that time is no barrier for those with Dragonskills, and as a result, these events are spread across the history of different realms, and some, in other instalments, are happening today.

However, I will say one thing. Look only a few decades into the future as it stands, and these events no longer take place. In fact, entire races may be lost by the time this tale is complete.

All that is really left for me to say right now is that I sincerely hope the first death of the series does not distress you. It is not up to me to dictate who lives and who dies? The person in question dug his own grave via his actions and while the grief remains for a long while to come, we must all learn to move on and accept our losses. There are many more to come and we will be in a pitiful state if we cannot bury our emotions and keep moving forward.

May the Elements guide you.
Hannah Chacko
Documenter of events that led to realm collapse and realm safety.

<u>Excerpt from The Destiny Records (many years before the first realm collapsed)</u>

<u>23rd November, fourth realm - by Xanja Hôder</u>

The new realm has now been established, and as a result, many races have come together to settle.

There are very distinct separations between races on this new world, few choosing to mingle. Already, some have obtained a sort of dominance over the others and have a new collective name for themselves: Humans. All races with similar shapes have converged. The Dracona have lost their ability to morph and have taken over one area of the world. The Mühans have taken over several larger areas and are already becoming more diverse among themselves. Many from Cyphia have travelled there, but their extreme diversity complicates their existence and already there are many smaller creatures appearing as they adapt to their new home. Very few Cyphans are 'humanoid'. It is the Prunœns and the Catréans who have become most dominant, and they can be found almost anywhere. The Raamé inhabit the dark places and already appear to be becoming creatures of legend. It will be most interesting to see how this realm develops and how so many co-exist.

How they have succeeded in creating a realm still remains a mystery, but this will hopefully not be the case for much longer. We have successfully planted a Watcher in the government departments of the second realm and he has gained access to the relevant files. The Prunœns, however, are easily suspicious and he is proceeding with caution. The details should be received via the Link in the near future.

Though they have only been settled for a year, the people are already renouncing their origins, making themselves believe that the memories they have are merely legends. A whole false history has been created to explain away the past. The first children to have been born have been taken into this woven web of lies, and it would appear to be the case that they are genuinely losing all recollection of their former lives. Time moves quickly on Earth. Quicker than any other realm.

The humans have also taken it upon themselves to disassociate themselves with magick, choosing instead to invent various substitutes, many of which could solve problems encountered by people in other realms. These new creations, known to the inhabitants as 'science' and 'technology' can overcome many barriers that our petty magicks cannot, and it would be well worth investigating their adaptability into our own lives. The best part is, these sciences do not drain the user's energy. They can be used indefinitely, despite illness or fatigue.

This lack of magick may be the main cause of the deteriorating association to the inhabitant's past lives. Magick defines us and is vital to our existence. This new realm will prove very useful towards understanding.

It is my personal belief that opening a

The Elementalists Series

Gate here in a few years time would be a breach of the Treaty. As the Gate Laws state, no realm is to be approached if the inhabitants are unaware of the Gates. They must come to us, like all realms that make themselves known. If absolutely necessary, then we may open a Gate in the isolated regions, i.e. the deserts and ice-caps. A map with their locations is accompanying this report. There are many unpopulated areas should people choose to visit the realm. Also, we are looking into planting Gatemen in other, more populated areas, so that Gates may be opened safely and without fear of discovery.

    Moving on from the fourth-realm, Cloric is becoming a dangerous place to travel through, and we may need to suspend all lines through the seventh realm.
    The Clorans themselves remain a peaceful race, but other beings are entering Cloric to fight their battles and not damage their own homes. The Clorans themselves can do little to stop this and refuse to take sides. Such invasions to this pure realm may prove problematic and I

suggest a team watch the realm at all times. There are too many new variables now and the Clorans rarely venture outside of their realm and they have little or no immunity to the afflictions of the realms. We cannot say what will happen to the race or the realm. The effects on other realms could prove just as ruinous.

The first prophecy is also worrying me, for it should not be long now until something catastrophic happens. We have no more than three decades before we will be forced to act on our intelligence. I advise the Clan Council to call a Gathering. We may be able to turn events on themselves, for the prophecy, as far as is known, bodes ill for us.

I have also recently been informed of misconduct within another team. I cannot list names here, but a messenger will be sent directly with the complete list. It is our duty to eliminate any problems before they get worse. We have a reputation among the realms which must be upheld.

The Elementalists Series

The Destiny Halls will be accessed shortly by a·certain Khexan: Havlerø Samx. We must make contact with the Oracles to alert them to the situation. He is to be given a full copy of the prophecy he requests and he is not to leave the room until he has handed the whole copy back. He is likely to try and take one or two pages with him; he is not to have any paper in or out of that room. This information must stay confined. Ensure he signs the Oath of Secrecy.

A team is in place in the fourth realm to continue reports with regard to the development of a new realm. It may be that they did not renounce their magick but lost touch with it by binding themselves somewhere new. The team will be withdrawn within five years as time runs on the realm in question.

Captain Xanja Hôder, reconnaissance squadron - 194, official recorder of all concerning the prophecies.

Prologue

He emerges from the Gate into the growing darkness. Looking around, all he sees is destruction. All he wants to do is turn back and find his son. He has done what was required before the Gathering and is now making his way to the dark halls of the clan.

Stiffening his resolve, he begins to pick his way through the rubble that has not yet vanished to the Wastelands. The roar of the Gate is still clear and it takes all he has not to turn back. Gradually, the sounds die and the empty town is filled with silence, like much of Vantrörkî. The Shadow-realm looks more desolate than ever. The armies have clearly been called away and everyone else should theoretically be at Gathering.

Knowing it will take a long time to get to Gathering in solid form, he merges with the intact shadow. Anything broken will soon disperse into the Wastelands and it is best he is not a part of it when that happens. In this state, he is no more than thought and shadow, moving silently and comparably quicker.

Why? he thinks, his pure form responding automatically to the Call. What could possibly have happened that merits Gathering? I could go and find my son. No one would know. *But in his shadowy heart, he knows that they will. He has to follow the Call or face the punishment for disobeying. Even so, there had been no word from his son. No message of safety. Many had already presumed the team lost to the Wastelands.*

Maybe I could detour, *he thinks slowly, looking around. I hear the Wastelands are pleasant at this time of year.* But he knows that is not the case. *The Wastelands are as close to hell as it is possible to get, yet all things lost turn up there, and sometimes, young Vertex get trapped, not knowing the way out, left as prey for the Beast.*

Mentally sighing, he reaches for a broken shadow soon to pass to the Wastelands, and he rests. This rushing around is rather tiring. I think I will wait here for a moment before continuing, *and he smiles in his hidden way.*

After a few moments, he feels the familiar tug of the dispersion. As the broken shadow is cast into the Wastelands, he cannot move.

After the portal's turbulence, he stands up in the dangerous Wastelands. Listening hard, he hears nothing. It is safe ... as safe as the Wastelands get. But he has to move quickly to avoid finding trouble. Carefully, he takes a solid form and gazes around. It seems even worse than the last time he was here. Towards one end, great fires rage on, never ceasing. Towards the other, shadows can be seen frozen in time. Either direction is perilous; only the centre is suitable to travel.

And so he searches, and his mind thinks back on earlier memories.

Darkness

A young boy ran towards me, arms outstretched. 'Father, Father,' he cried.

I looked at him, my face blank before recognition took it. So much time had passed and the lad was almost ready. His mother would have been proud if she were around to see. I opened my arms and let him run into my embrace. I was home.

I looked around the familiar darkness, my son following my gaze. He took my hand and led me off, pulling me away to show me the meal he made. This, I realised, is no place to raise a child. And so I looked at his face, so light and warm. Staying here would darken his heart to the shadow that holds the rest of us. We had to leave. If only for his sake…

He is jerked back to reality as a slight movement catches his eye. He stares into the darkness, trying to see what caused the flicker of shadow on shadow. A fleeting shape comes into view, only to disappear once more. The movement brings back even earlier memories, before his wife had died.

We travelled to the second realm. A place of peace. Vlökir ran back and forth, exploring the new environment. I turned to her, captured, as always, by her beauty.

'He will be a fine young Vertex. You know that?' she whispered to me.

I nodded once, his form flitting past as he spent his

excess energy. My fear was he would become too good, and be recruited.

She put a comforting arm around me, smiling. She knew what that life had done to me ... what it was still doing to me. I could not allow my only son to be ensnared by the Clan's politics.

He pauses, having heard the smallest of voices. He strains his ears, trying to hear more. Sure enough, it is a child's voice. Trapped in the Wastelands. He quickens his pace, sure it is his son. Fearful that he is already too late.

He approaches the source of the sound slowly; unsure of what he will find when he looks. Steeling himself, he glances into the pit. A young boy gazes up at him, his eyes filled with fear.

'Help me father.'

The man lowers himself into the pit. It is not deep, but the sides are steep and the boy is too small to reach the top. The man helps his son from the pit before pulling himself out.

'How many times have I told you?' he asks sternly.

The boy looks up sheepishly. 'I didn't know. I don't remember what happened.'

The roar of a Gate comes from behind them. A young woman steps out, ensuring the Gate remains open.

'You are late. The Clan is waiting.'

Taking his son's hand, the man steps through the Gate. The woman shakes her head and follows, shutting it behind them.

Darkness falls,
Darkness rises.
This world is shrouded with shadow.

The light will fade.
I am coming.

Chapter 1

He Broke His Oath Today

Daesir wandered through the camp alone. It was a warm night and he could find no rest. No matter how hard he had tried, sleep avoided him completely. So instead of lying in bed awake, he had decided to walk in the fresh air to see if it helped in any way.

The camp was deserted; the evening crew had already been dismissed, leaving behind them a calming silence.

But despite the soothing touch of the night, Daesir could not feel at ease. Something was going to happen that night, and whatever it was, it would not be good. Someone would die that night. He could feel it, but could not understand his feeling.

He heard voices shouting over a roaring sound

somewhere in the camp. One of the voices belonged to Mattias. He began to run towards the sound, praying that he was not too late.

Another voice became audible. It was shouting something furiously. Shouting frantically until it was suddenly cut off.

In that moment, Daesir was sure he knew exactly what he would find.

* * * * * * * * * * * *

It had been several days since Scarien had taught them to control their skills, and both Mattias and Camer were growing restless. That morning, Scarien had told them he could teach them no more and that they would leave that evening, giving them time to make their farewells. They had learnt much over the past few days, and were beginning to feel stifled when they both knew they could be doing more good elsewhere.

Both boys walked through the camp for the umpteenth time, neither saying a word, nor communicating through thought. They were looking forward to setting off, but at the same time, they were unhappy at the prospect of leaving all they knew behind.

In particular, all their friends would be staying at the camp. They would be travelling alone. It would be an adventure, but it would probably be a lonely one.

'Mattias!' Lyana called as they walked past, and she jogged up to meet them. 'I hear you're leaving,' she said in her normal soft tones.

Mattias nodded glumly. 'Yeah,' he sighed, looking up at her. 'I've been trying to find you. Scarien will need someone in charge while he is away. He left the appointment up to us.' He paused, glancing at Camer who nodded once. 'We would like you to take the post.'

Lyana was lost for words. She had not expected anything of the sort, and somewhat doubted their decision. 'Are you sure? I mean, do you think…' she paused, taking in the expressions on the boys' faces. 'Well…' she started, 'if you insist.'

Mattias unpinned his badge and handed it to her. 'You'll do a better job than I ever could.'

She smiled briefly. 'Good luck, Both of you. This badge will be waiting for your return.'

'I don't know if we will be able to return,' Camer said grimly, 'Our road leads far from this place, and we might…'

'But we will try.' Mattias interrupted quickly.

Lyana nodded briefly and hugged both the boys. She smiled faintly and whispered another good luck. Carefully pinning the badge to her top she nodded a final farewell to them both and walked slowly back to her post to resume work.

The boys watched her go for several moments, realising once again just how much they were leaving behind, before turning away and continuing their walk.

* * * * * * * * * * * *

Night fell and the pair were waiting at the edge of the camp, looking rather forlorn on their own. Each had a medium-sized rucksack containing spare clothes, a small food supply, a blanket, and a few precious belongings. Everything else they owned was left in Mattias's room, which they had locked, just in case there was a possibility of their future return to the camp.

Mattias looked out into the growing darkness once again. Straining his eyes against the gloom, he could just about make out a figure walking towards them. Despite the poor light and the distance between them, Mattias knew instantly that it was his father. It was something about the way he walked and the aura about him.

As he drew nearer, Scarien breathed a hidden sigh of relief. He had been fearful for their safety and was sure something had happened between that morning and the present moment.

He paused, contemplating his decision to aid them directly. It broke his Oath completely. But the odds were stacked high against them. If he did not help them, in whatever way he could, everything could be lost. He had only pushed his bonds thus long, now it was time to break them and reap the consequences.

Once he was near enough to the pair, he pulled something out of his pocket. Without the slightest hint of regret, he handed it to Camer. 'This was for Vyus to wear, but is Caya's. Wear it until such a time that you regain your own. The four of you will need to exchange them for the correct pendants.'

Camer took it carefully and looked at it. On a fine gold chain hung a translucent, silver eagle, with markings that appeared to be in white paint.

Mattias glanced at it and pulled out the pendant that hung from his neck. It was identical in properties, but instead of being an eagle, it was a snake, and it was green in colour. 'This would be your one. Earth,' he stated, realising what they represented for the first time.

Scarien nodded. 'You have always been observant, Mattias, but don't swap them now. Find your sisters first. Only swap them when the time is right. You must all be together.'

Camer fastened the chain about his neck and tucked it out of sight. Mattias casually hid his own under his shirt once more.

Scarien nodded approvingly before then handing Mattias an envelope. 'Just in case,' he said simply.

Mattias tucked it into a pocket, next to the letter Scarien had given him on his birthday. He was curious as to what it contained, but knew his father well enough not to ask. He hoped that he would not have to read it. The words, 'Just in case', were ominous.

The three looked at each other, assuring themselves that they were ready. Checking once again that they had everything they would need, they began their journey.

* * * * * * * * * * * *

They had barely begun to leave the camp when a deafening sound came from behind them. It was like a roaring wind gushing through their ears.

'A Gate!' shouted Scarien, his fears realised all too

soon. 'This way. Hurry!'

He began to lead the boys away quickly, but the sound became no less distant. He had hoped for more time, but the letter was all that was needed. There was now no escape from whatever was coming through from another realm, but still they ran.

After a while, Scarien stopped, resigned. The boys were tiring fast, realising how unfit they had become. With anxious eyes, the man looked around, knowing what had come through but wondering where they were.

A man clad in sliver, black and white robes stepped through into the realm. The Gate was invisible, yet the sound was all too audible. More similarly-robed men and women followed until eleven had come through in total. The group of newcomers surrounded the trio. They gave off an aura that made them seem 'wrong', as though they should never have existed.

These people had a rather strange appearance. Their robes hung down to their feet, and almost covered their hands on the outside of the sleeve. Their skin was silvery-grey, their hair black. Each of them wore the same, emotionless expression, with extremely angled features.

'Scarien Éscaronôvic,' said the first man softly, his voice somehow echoing above the noise of the Gate. The other arrivals hissed in anticipation, the sound filled with malice. The man smiled and held up a hand to still them. 'We are the Oathkeepers. You made an Oath on your life exactly eighteen years ago. You kept that Oath well for those eighteen years. You bent the rules around your Oath well. But now that Oath is broken. We come today to collect the debt you owe us.'

The Oathkeepers smiled venomously, their red eyes flashing hungrily. The tension in the air grew, suffocating the trio as they closed in.

Mattias blinked in confusion for several moments before suddenly comprehending what it was they were saying. 'No!' he shouted, barely hearing himself over the roar of the Gate. 'You can't do that!'

The man, the Oathkeeper looked at him. 'It is our duty, our sole purpose of existence. We must claim the debts created by broken Oaths. In this particular case, we gave him plenty of allowances, considering the circumstances, but a broken Oath cannot be overlooked,' he said, almost apologetically, yet evil seemed to ring through his voice.

Camer shouted something inaudible in his own tongue, prompting the man to turn to him instead. 'How touching. But I am afraid I cannot be swayed so easily. You would do well to keep your tongue behind your teeth, Shadow. *Hes'varon chrx grtauzh.* Now, please keep quiet unless you have something constructive to say.'

Note to readers:

Indeed it will seem to you all that the Oathkeepers are evil and heartless beings. While they may be heartless, it would be better to think of their functioning as being similar to a machine's. A machine will always complete tasks in specific ways. They cannot break the rules of their programming. For example, pressing the letter 'a' on a keyboard, when typing, will produce the letter 'a' on screen where the cursor is. Should the system not follow the rules set down, who can say what letter will appear? The letter 'a' could be a 'j' on screen, or even a 'y', and it is unlikely to be consistent.

In machines, consistency is vital. The Oathkeepers are the same. They were created for one reason: to collect the debts created by broken Oaths. If they did not, what would be the point of saying: 'I swear on my life...'? Those words would have no meaning.

Unlike machines, however, the Oathkeepers are conscious. But when your race's survival depends on you following the rules, I am sure you would all do the same thing.

In addition, for those curious readers, the language the Oathkeeper spoke in, and also the one Camer uses in just a moment, is the language of Vantrörkî. For those who enjoy learning extra, the language is also known as Vötra.

To resume:

Camer fell silent and glanced at Mattias, linking up to his friend's mind in an instant. ~*This cannot happen.* Kh'sarx zaph'rm. We need *Scarien. How else will we manage to do anything?*~

~*I know. There has to be something we can do.*~

The man laughed. 'Do not think your thoughts go unheard children. We hear all, spoken or not. You can do nothing. Our existence is brought about for only one reason. Our eternal lives hold only one purpose.'

All the Oathkeepers hissed a verse, reciting it as a child would from a book. They repeated it over and over, filling all hearts nearby with dread.

'You make the Oaths.

'We hear them.

'You state the price of failure.

'We hear it.

'The Oathkeepers know through all time and space.

'You break the Oaths.

'We know this.

'You owe a debt.

'We collect it.

'The Äescardïonas keep the Oaths and exist to collect that which you say you'll pay.

'You make the Oaths.

'We hear them...'

Their voices were like that of a never-ending nightmare, full of meaning in a way most would rather not understand. As they spoke, they tightened the circle around the trio, all gaps filling quickly. There could be no escape.

Scarien shouted to the boys. At first his words were lost in the din, but he raised his voice so they could hear him. 'Find the girls and save the Vertex. The pendants ... the inheritance chains ... they fit into the Zynoran. You will know how when the time is right.

'I'm so proud of you ... both of you. You, Mattias, are truly my son ... and Camer, you are the son I lost years ago ... the son I never knew. Become who you are destined to be ... show them all ... I believe in you. The answers are in Dra'noxia. Remember...'

His voice was suddenly drowned out by the Oathkeepers, cut off as if someone had pressed a mute button on him. All the boys could hear were the voices of the Oathkeepers and the deafening sound of the still-open Gate.

The circle now held only Scarien, the boys somehow left on the outside, although they could not recall being passed by the Oathkeepers. Both shouted to him, only to hear their voices whipped away into the mix of noise. The volume grew and grew, threatening to burst their ears.

And suddenly it was silent. In front of them, the boys could still see the Oathkeepers ringed around Scarien, though they could no longer see the man himself, and they could see that they were still hissing the dreadful words. The Gate was still open, and they knew that the sound must still be there, but they heard nothing. Just an eerie silence.

At first, Mattias thought he was deaf until a long, constant sound could be heard, a humming sound, like a note was being held on a wind instrument. It was so high, that both boys had to cover their ears to try and block it out, but to no avail. It drilled through their skulls agonisingly.

A white, blinding light pierced the darkness and the boys instinctively shielded their eyes. The silence continued for less than a second longer before all was still. The night was once again calm, the breeze blowing gently across their faces. Night-time sounds were audible once more and there was no trace of the Oathkeepers. It was all

Darkness

over: the Gate was closed and the Oathkeepers gone.

As their eyes adjusted to the sudden darkness, the boys heard a whisper over in the breeze. *Oathbreaker, your debt has been paid.*

A motionless figure lay in the dirt. Mattias ran over, tears in his eyes, shouting in disbelief, already knowing what had happened. Camer simply walked behind, numb.

When he reached his father's body, Mattias fell to his knees. 'No...' he choked, unable to come to terms with what had just happened seconds before.

At first, he clasped an already icy hand before letting it drop to the ground. To the bereaved boy, it seemed to fall in slow motion, hitting the ground with an unnaturally loud thump, amplified by the night's stillness. Mattias then cradled Scarien's head, burying his face in the well-kept hair. As the events began to hit home, Mattias wept, his tears falling freely, only to be soaked up by the mass of black hair.

Camer crouched next to and slightly behind him, comforting him for both their sakes. Unsure of what to say, he managed to whisper, 'We couldn't do anything to help ... we couldn't do anything.' His voice held little of his pain and he tried to keep it from showing on his face, but inside he ran the same thought through over and over: *He's gone ... he's really gone ... Scarien is gone ... we're alone ...*

they took him ... he's really gone...

Look at all the children.
They see the world in colour.
Magick is everywhere.

They do not see the darkness.
They only see the wonder.
The light.

Chapter 2

The Finals and the Facts

After six successful rounds, Qwenox had managed to scrape their way into the finals. Qyan's logic proved that change was sometimes for the better, and Caya's strategies made the idea a reality. Without her mind fuelling their tactics, their successes would never have been possible.

After being told the task that they would have to complete, both finalists were given two days to prepare. Caya had quickly begun to work on a strategy and then a back-up plan in case of any complications. As they ran through each, the team smoothed out any flaws, accommodating for all possibilities. They could win this as long as it all went smoothly. They rehearsed so many different scenarios that most of them could not imagine what could possibly go wrong.

'Qwenox. Enter the arena.'

The voice sounded throughout the entire village, alerting to all that the finals were about to begin. The team entered, walking briskly, lead by Xanor and Haero. Behind them came Qyan and Caya; then Nesqo and Scortia. Finally, Barek and Iano brought up the rear. Each was dressed in their tournament robes - red and gold for Fire, black and blue for Water, light-blue and silver for Air and brown and green for Earth.

As they entered the arena, they gazed around, the stands quickly filling with spectators once more. Almost everyone had shown up to watch the event. After all, the finals were always the most exciting challenge.

'Dracör. Enter the arena.'

The opposing team entered in the same order of elements. They lined up opposite Qwenox and hissed insults at them, a common psycho-out technique.

'Welcome to the finals Qyan,' smirked one of the boys, also clad in black. 'This must be a new experience for you. After all, you *are* usually wiped out in the first round. Everyone started going easy on poor Qwenox.'

Qyan and Caya half glanced at each other and remained silent, allowing the taunts to wash over them without caring. After all, they knew the team well enough to know that they were normally very nice people. It was a shame that competition affected them so.

'It doesn't matter anyway. You won't be here for long. We've wiped the floor with our opponents every year. A bunch of rookies won't stop us from winning yet again.'

Qyan smiled, a rare occurrence for the Water Elementalist. As a result, the expression appeared strange on his normally solemn face. 'You may very well defeat us, as you do many others every year. But we have something worth more than any tournament trophy,' he said, raising his voice slightly so that the whole team could all hear. 'We have a connection running deeper than any other can know. Such a feat cannot be achieved by those with hearts set on the prize. Only by those who have their hearts set on helping each other to be the very best they can be.' He fell silent, saying no more, leaving the other team stunned by his words.

~Nice one Qyan,~ complimented Xanor. ~Hit them in their pride. As long as they think that we have something that they don't, they'll be unable to focus.~

~But we do have something that they do not,~ commented Qyan matter-of-factly. ~I did not lie to them.~

~Never mind,~ Xanor muttered before addressing the team as a whole. ~Now, does everyone know what it is they are *meant to do?~*

A general affirmative ran through the minds of the team, accompanied by a slight groan. They had gone through the plan far too many times to be forgetting it in a hurry, but Xanor insisted they keep going over every detail, time and time again. Competition also appeared to go to his head. He was desperate not to lose.

~Remember girls: don't even attempt a full strike. A weakened blow leaves you both unconscious as it is. Anyway, we don't want to be disqualified for using terminal force,~ Barek reminded them.

Caya frowned, *~Wouldn't killing them be worse than the disqualification?~*

Scortia mentally grinned and sent a nudge to Caya, her expression not showing how funny she had found that. *~Don't tempt me Barek. I might get carried away. Anyway, on a serious note, does everyone remember plan B?~*

The rest of the team groaned again. Plan B had been rehearsed so many times that it was drilled into them. Even more so than plan A. Scortia made them run through it repeatedly, for she was not keen on the idea that winning relied solely on her and Caya. It was far too much pressure for her and this was her way of coping.

'You have all been given instructions. But, just in case any of you have forgotten, I will repeat them. The finals consist of one round. A battle, solely fought by magick. All opponents must be unconscious for the champions to be declared,' called the voice once more. 'No terminal force is to be used, intentionally or otherwise. Failure to follow these rules will result in immediate disqualification.'

Someone from the audience called out, clearly audible. 'But how can they not use terminal force if they do so unintentionally. Accidents happen.' This statement prompted much muttering amongst all spectators, as it did every year. The challenges were always similar in nature.

~*Fair comment.*~ said Qyan, thinking it over with a sly thought-expression.

~*Honestly. Only you Qyan. That question is just going to make us stand here forevermore and increase the desernas now fluttering uncomfortably in my stomach.*~ said Caya, shaking her head slowly.

Note to readers:

I apologise for the notes I have been providing, but I am sure it would be a disservice to simply relay the tale rather than providing snippets of information. This seems to be the best, and most personal way, to provide this information.

Desernas are creatures of Catré that resemble those we know as butterflies. However, they also have a nice sting to them when angered. It contains a mild neurotoxin.

To resume:

Xanor laughed. ~*Quit it you two. This may very well be relevant. You can bite each other's heads off later.*~

The team turned their attention to the voices. The announcer was consulting the high-councillors before replying. 'If terminal force is used, the wielder will be taken immediately to Council and the team disqualified. There, they will make a statement in the old tongue, binding as it is. If indeed it was accidental, they will be automatically removed from all future tournaments on the basis that they are a threat to other competitors and will be given extensive training, in solitude, until they are deemed safe to be reintroduced to society. If they cannot be rehabilitated, then the resulting threat will be removed permanently. If terminal force is used and is deemed intentional, the wielder will be executed immediately to remove the threat to the safety of the people.'

A few minutes passed after this statement, allowing it to sink in. The judges took this time to take their positions and add a few notes to the papers in front of them. As soon as they were seated, the four officials raised a force-field, able to keep all the blows within the arena and acted as sound-proofing on the competitors' behalves, allowing for full concentration. Only then did the commentators pick up the pace, their voices barred to the two teams lest it provide an unfair advantage.

The call to take up their starting positions came and Dracör formed their customary diamond instantly. The formation was simple, yet effective, having never been breached to date. The two points closest and furthest from their opponents were covered by Water. The left-front and right-back sides were by Fire and the other sides were by Earth. The two remaining positions were protected by Air. Each team member shielded themselves and two others giving their defence three strong layers. This also allowed them to maintain defences while attack their opponents.

Qwenox formed two squares, one inside the other. Each square had one person from each element making up the corners. Those on the outside were delegated the task of maintaining the defences without any breaches. The shields were raised by Xanor, Qyan, Nesqo and Barek. Iano and Haero were in charge of keeping their opponents attention and served as the distraction for the main strike. Caya and Scortia readied themselves to unleash a force not unlike that which had previously floored Nesqo and Qyan, only they had managed to strengthen the strike greatly through training.

~Their shields do not cover the top. From about ten metres

up, they are unprotected,~ said Qyan, having examined the opposing defences. *~Haero, Iano. Attack their sides repeatedly to keep them occupied. With a bit of luck, they will be distracted enough to ignore the rest of us.*

~Scortia, Caya. Raise your attack as high as you can without attracting attention. If you can get over their defences then the majority of the strike will be contained by their own shields. Remember to weaken it enough so that you do not risk killing them. Unconscious is what we want.

~Everyone else, our defences must *be maintained and strong. At the same time we need to be able to hold them under any attack. It would be best if we could all detach. We would then be able to cover all sides with four layers, plus it would enable us to strike without lowering shields.~*

Everyone immediately took a meditative position and detached themselves from their bodies. It was much easier to do now compared to the first time they used it as they had practiced intensely since the maze. This way, their bodies were merely markers for which to focus their shields while they were free to spread their magick much further. In addition to that, more strength could be used in their magick, as they did not need to devote so much energy into keeping their bodies active.

'On my mark,' came the call, ringing loudly within the battlefield. 'Three. Two. One. *Santörÿ.*'

As soon as the restrictions on attacking magick were lifted, Qwenox struck hard. Dracör were kept behind their defences as their shields were pounded. There was no chance for them to counter-attack. Iano and Haero dealt blow after blow, their magick flying from all directions. This also served to minimise the view both teams had of the field, covering Scortia and Caya's work.

After several minutes, Iano spoke, the strain becoming apparent. *~Now would be a good time girls. We can't keep this up forever and a day.~*

They had been attacking hard, but their attacks were becoming weaker as their strength ebbed, Haero, barely inflicting any damage now.

The girls looked at each other, both with the same thought in mind. *It is too soon.* They had not managed to muster enough energy to provide an effective attack. They could not waste this strike, for there would not be a second chance.

~Haero, Iano. Cease fire and reserve your energy,~ said Qyan. *~Count out slowly to ninety before you try to attack again. Don't attack hard, though. Just give them enough to keep them busy.~*

The two boys obliged, counting out the numbers as Dracör used the gap to throw all they had at their opponents. Qwenox defences, however, held well.

~Now!~ the girls signalled, ready to convert their energy to their attack.

Haero and Iano used all they had left to bombard Dracör, forcing the team back behind their shields. Caya and Scortia closed their eyes, letting the magick build up inside them with increasing pressure.

While the attack was being prepared, Qwenox dropped all defences and gave Dracör all they had, keeping all attention on them, rather than the girls. They needed to give the girls the time to strike. Should Dracör focus on the coming attack, they could prevent the pair from discharging the magick.

As the pressure became too great to withstand, the girls released the force, which shot upwards, over Dracör's defences. It arched towards the ground and impacted with enough force to shatter all the shields, filling the field.

The shield protecting the spectators also fell, the audience feeling the wave of energy rush over them. Fortunately, the magick was harmless by the time it reached them.

It was all over ... almost. Qyan saw that one of the opponents had escaped the blast, focussing his shield around himself. Conjuring a small ball of water, Qyan threw it as hard as he could, and it smacked into the boy's

Darkness

head. Unconsciousness was immediate.

Caya and Scotia had also fallen unconscious, their strength drained by the force of their attack. Lending them a portion of their remaining energy, the rest of the team got the girls back on their feet.

Healers were running into the arena and checking the injuries of the fallen Dracör. After a few agonising minutes, one nodded to the commentator before setting about the Healing process to provide the team with enough energy.

'Qwenox wins!' came the announcement, cheers filling the stadium.

The crowd surged forward into the arena, everyone looking to congratulate their champions. Dracör had been undefeated for so long, that Qwenox were sure to be the talk of the village for the next few months.

Jared pushed his way over, through the swarms of people. He was clearly concerned for the girls, who were unable to stand unsupported. They were still shaking and were rather weak, which was a normal side-effect of the pressure they had been under. Despite allowing it to build up to dangerous levels, they were recovering quickly and smiled as he approached.

Caya found her balance and waved Qyan away. He stood slightly behind her, ready in case she fell; she still looked unsteady.

'I'm fine.' she said, not bothering to raise her voice over the thundering crowd, her face regaining colour as she grinned at their victory.

* * * * * * * * * * * *

Dracör had regained consciousness quickly with the help of the Healers, and were once again lined up opposite Qwenox. The two teams shook hands and congratulated each other on a good match before the trophy was passed from the old champions to the new.

After this traditional ceremony, the two teams wandered off to the training halls together, knowing the garden would be empty thanks to their battle. Once there, they immediately began to talk about the final round.

Several minutes into their discussion, one of the older members of Dracör said, ~*How? That's what I fail to understand. It's worked for so long.*~

Scortia smiled. ~ *Everything has to fail at some point. We spread the attacks and defences between all team members and worked to discover your main weaknesses,*~ she said. She then added, ~*You didn't defend from above and your defences were also too thin to resist our main strike. That was the weakness we exploited,*~ in response to Dracör's bemused faces.

Caya then said. ~*Our other attacks were merely intended to distract you. If you had realised what we were doing, it would never have worked.*~

Both teams then entered a general discussion, steering away from the tournament to get away from the pressure both teams had felt. It was time for them to move along. The boy who had attempted to insult Qyan earlier, however, offered his apologies first before changing the topic, allowing both teams to begin to feel at ease. It was pleasant to talk without all the competitive tensions they had felt before.

Suddenly, Caya felt a sense of loss; a hole had been torn in her heart. She felt the tears flow freely down her face, but could not explain them. Someone close to her had died, but she did not know who. The feeling was instinctive and she sensed that two others, far away, felt the same. She glanced at Scortia through blurry eyes and saw that she was in the same state, feeling the same loss.

~*What's the matter?*~ asked Iano, noticing their obvious pain.

All faces turned to them and the next thing the girls knew, they were in the middle of a comforting group hug. Everyone was asking what was wrong, trying to comfort the pair.

~*Xanor,*~ said Caya, keeping her thought voice

steady. ~*Do you know that prophecy in full? It may be slightly relevant. I felt two others, close to us, weeping for the same reasons. Maybe there is some connection.*~

Xanor nodded and the group turned to him, the garden seeming appropriately silent, ready and waiting for a long tale to be told.

~*Just so you all know, I heard this by accident and it is not meant to be repeated. It is one of those forbidden tales and it is unlikely that you will ever hear it repeated again.*~ And so he cast a small fire on the ground in front of him as he began to recite the tale, as he had heard it. As he did so, the fire began to display the story with vivid golden images. ~*Long before our time, the Clorans thrived in their own realm, a promising and necessary race to all…*~

Their realm was known as Cloric and was the seventh amongst the known. In its time, it was the most splendid of all those known at the time. It was split into nine great cities, dressed up in a white stone, not dissimilar to marble.

Between each of the cities stretched vast expanses of unbroken, untouched wild land. The Clorans, though urban-dwellers themselves, were utterly at peace with the nature surrounding them, living in harmony with their realm.

Of the cities, one stood out amongst them: in the centre of the realm stood Tresh, capital of Cloric. Though more work had been put into crafting its beauty than had been anywhere else, this was not the distinguishing feature, for above it was situated the Citadel of Tresh. If times of war or hardship came, and they did so frequently due to tensions between other realms, the citadel could house every Cloran in the realm with room to spare, such was its size. It was crafted from impregnable, resilient rock and gleamed brightly in the light of the realm.

~In contrast with the brilliant white of-~
~Please Xanor, get to the point,~ interrupted Haero, already bored of the irrelevant details.
~Wait, I'm getting there. The background makes it a good story to tell and is somewhat relevant, I think. Now, where was I? Oh yes. The citadel was crafted from impregnable, resilient rock. In contrast with the brilliant white of the cities...~

...it was a deep sapphire blue, and even those who weren't of Cloric could easily lose themselves in its splendour; its surface would capture the eye and ensnare the mind with swirling patterns.

However, the Clorans, though they perceived it as their sanctuary, began to realise the dangers of grouping their race together and began the building of other citadels, all ruby red. They were optimistic at the progress of the project and worked quickly. This would allow each city population to be protected *and also allowed the Clorans to reach a Citadel quickly. Before, they would have had to travel to the centre of the realm each time Outsiders threatened.*

However, months into their work, one Cloran predicted an imminent danger would come to their realm, threatening the lives of every Cloran, young and old. Instinctively, every Cloran made their way to the Citadel of Tresh. Supplies were brought with each person to last for months. If they were kept out of the realm for longer, the tunnels provided access to the outside.

The growing regularity of war caused them to expect an attack on this occasion. However, they failed to anticipate the diseases carried by the invaders. Usually, the diseases were wiped out by the sheer volume of magick in the realm, but one mutated rapidly enough to overcome the boundaries. This deadly virus attacked the Clorans, who had never before had the need for a cure of any kind. Having never experienced illness, the Clorans had no immunity and the experience was new and terrifying. Once it was seen that the disease was clearly contagious, they all fled to the tunnels with a desire to escape.

But there was no way out. As the death toll rose, the tunnels became blocked and the Gates to and from the realm crumbled. Realm-jumping became impossible. They were trapped and picked off one by one by the killer virus. Those the disease did not affect were forced to sit and watch their realm crumble around them, a death more cruel than the pain the virus caused.

Darkness

It is believed that eventually, the disease was destroyed. Regardless, the survivors were beyond saving.

Unknown to most other realms, a small band of survivors had escaped. About eleven became known to the Elementalists. The others, if any others had survived, disappeared from knowledge and theories state they suffered from trauma-induced amnesia, allowing them to integrate into other realms as though they had lived among them all their lives.

One of the group in contact with the Elementalists was on the brink of death and, in his last hour, revealed a prophecy he had Seen not four days before the realm collapsed.

'From a Letran and Zyron will be born four children with the power to end all wars and save all realms, known and unknown. They will become the only hope for existence, if any wish to survive.

'They will control all elements as their own and will share a bond so deep that injury and emotion are all shared, affecting them, even when they do not know it should. They will be placed among different families in the sixth realm, their true identities hidden from them and all around them. Whenever one perishes, he or she must be replaced with another Dragonsoul.

'Each will have an inheritance chain that belongs to another, and this will allow the four to be drawn together. The answers they seek lie in Dra'noxia, and it is there that they will come together after many years of their lives. Their first

challenge will come soon after and their success will determine their own survival, along with that of many others.

'Once the realms no longer need them, they will pass from existence and all knowledge. Before that time can come, many will try to sway them. These people believe that possessing the children will allow them to move the realms in the direction they wish. However, it is the choices that the children make that will be the true way. Their resolute choices determine the fates of all who live and ever have lived.

'As they grow in power, they will even have the ability to call back the Dead, creating life where it was never intended to remain. This power will separate them from all others and they will use it on more than one occasion before their time comes. Whether they use it in the right circumstances will determine their fate.

'They will also learn of three more with powers as great as their own. They may be the children central to our realms, but they are not the only ones. The Balance will manifest itself in an attempt to protect the realms. And there were six, not four, Great Ones. There must be two others.

'The Void must be feared and the shadows must be counted. As one realm falls, the stability lessens. The realms are needed to maintain order.'

After this, he gave the last Zynoran to the Letran leader, setting the prophecy in motion.

'This will fit their inheritance chains and will be an essential part of their future.'

They were the last words he spoke.

The fire image faded as Xanor finished. The tale was followed by a long silence which seemed louder than the Gate noise.

~*The prophecy was longer, but the first part didn't really concern you … at least, I don't believe it does. I cannot remember much of the rest,*~ Xanor added matter-of-factly.

~*So…*~ began Scortia after much deliberation. ~*We're sisters?*~

~*Twins in every way possible, other than the fact you were born the day after each other. The midnight stroke was all that separated you,*~ said Xanor. ~*I remember the Council discussing it, and how it could be no coincidence.*~

Caya nodded. It was beginning to make sense to her. ~*So what we felt must have been something, somewhere else. We were feeling what the others felt.*~ She paused. ~*It felt like someone really close had been lost … I wonder who it was though. The others were really distraught, putting us in the same state.*~ She remained pensive for a few more moments before dismissing her thoughts, the lost feeling fading fast. Standing, she smiled at the group. ~*Shall we?*~

The Balance has already shifted.
The realms are in turmoil.
It will not be long.

But something is missing.
More is needed.
The skies will turn black.

Chapter 3

The Gate of Flames

The Letran camp was in an uproar. News of Scarien's death had spread like wildfire and great confusion filled the minds of all the soldiers. Instinctively, they looked to Mattias, who was now their leader, but there was no leader to be found there. There was only a teenage boy, grieving for his father.

Lyana ran towards the growing crowd and, after pulling a couple of men aside and whispering something to them, she dispersed the onlookers. 'Go back to your stations. This place will not run itself!'

Watching them all leave again, she walked slowly towards Daesir, who was still shocked by the scene before him, ashamed for not arriving in time. She quickly whispered something to him and he nodded, retreating to his dormitory, head bowed.

She watched him go before walking up to the two boys. Camer looked at her, loss written all over his face and filling the boy's eyes. Yet still no tears fell to mirror his pain.

She placed a comforting hand on his shoulder, and he looked down again, sitting backwards, his arms around his knees. She sighed softly, watching him for a moment, wondering how she could help him. Unsure, she moved forwards towards a grieving Mattias. Gently, she tried to pull the boy off of his father.

At first, he struggled, not wishing to be separated from the father he had always known but only recently found. But soon, he relaxed into her embrace, tears falling freely from his eyes and down his already wet cheeks. His gaze never left his father's body, as if he were still wishing for him to get up again, knowing he never would.

Soothing him as a mother would a child, Lyana pulled him back away from Scarien and towards Camer. She nodded to the two men who were watching awkwardly. Between them, they carefully lifted the body and carried it respectfully away to the Tower of the Dead for burial preparation.

Camer just sat there, numb. He could not cry for his

pain was too great and came with loss and confusion. And thrown in for good measure was guilt, though in reality he had nothing to feel guilty about. But he felt as if he should have done more against the Oathkeepers.

Mattias eventually pulled free and wiped his face with his sleeve. A few stray tears remained, but he ignored them and moved closer to Camer, hugging his friend tight. The two boys remained motionless for some time, Camer still as lost as before. Mattias sighed and stood yet again, feeling the need to find some strength to keep going for Scarien would not have wanted them to grieve continually.

He then helped Camer to his feet, for he seemed incapable of getting up himself, frozen in place. Then, together, they made their steady way back to Scarien's office, Lyana following on behind.

The office, Mattias noticed, did not seem as welcoming as it had before, but somewhat colder and darker. But as nothing had changed about the room, he realised it was merely his perception of it that had changed.

It was missing Scarien's cheerful face in the doorway as they entered. It did not have the slightly agitated figure hidden by reams of paper, or sitting by the fire as he puzzled over something. No hot drinks were sitting around or being prepared, the empty mugs all stone cold. The fire had been reduced to a few burning embers and the sense of safety had disappeared altogether.

Nevertheless, it was still Scarien's office, as it was when the man was taking a well-earned holiday, or when some urgent business had called him away from the camp. It was a room waiting for its owner to return.

Only this time, he won't return. thought Mattias sadly. *That is what is different.*

Camer sat in his usual chair at the small table and stared at the place Scarien would usually fill, half-expecting and half-hoping the Letran to fill the space once again. The events seemed unreal, like a nightmare from which there was no escape. His disbelief blocked the grief from fully expressing itself.

He pulled out the eagle-pendant and stared at it almost unblinkingly, running Scarien's words through his head. *'This was for Vyus to wear, but is Caya's. Wear it until such a time that you regain your own. The four of you will need to exchange them for the correct pendants.'* Scarien saw him worthy of it ... no, more than that... *'Camer, you are the son I lost years ago ... the son I never knew.'* Scarien saw him as a son. He could ask for no higher praise than that. He felt honoured.

Mattias reached into his pocket and pulled out the

envelope Scarien had handed him. *'Just in case.'* Was this what his father had meant? He seemed to have known that the Oathkeepers were coming for him. Surely there was no other 'just in case' now. They had needed Scarien's guidance for the realms they would travel to and now, that help was gone.

He flipped the envelope over several times, wondering whether he should open it. He was afraid of what he might find inside, what Scarien might have said. Then again, he was afraid of what would happen if he did not open it; what he might do in the future should he not read its contents. They could end up far off track.

After some deliberation, he eased it open slowly. As he did so, he noted how thick it was, wondering how much could possibly be contained in a letter of a dead man.

Shaking open the sheets of paper, he read slowly. The first time through, he barely registered the words, instead staring at the familiar flowing script, which triggered new pain. But he blinked away the tears that were forming and began to read what his father had wished to say.

Dear Mattias and Camer,

If you are reading this letter, then it is as I feared, and expected if truth be told. The Oathkeepers, the Äescardionas to use their true name, are merciless and I was prepared to accept my fate. And so all I would have told you is contained in this letter, plus some extra advice should you find yourselves in other situations.

The first thing you must do is find your sisters. Head to Dra'noxia and you should find them there. The inheritance chains are drawing you all together. Once you find them, swap so that you have the chains that reflect your element. Seahorse for Water, salamander for Fire, snake for Earth and eagle for Air. Then break the Zynoran. The pendants will fit the correct element automatically. You will know how when the time comes.

Also in Dra'noxia, you will find the answers you need. You may not know the questions yet, but you will, in time. Look in the Destiny Halls and retrieve the prophecy numbered 11-9864-78533-54. Do not read it as it may seriously affect the course of the future. But keep it safe from prying eyes for others are moving to acquire it themselves. If you are asked for identification, repeat these words: 'A Cloran's sacrifice requires honour. An Elementalist's sacrifice requires love. Together prophecies are born.' If they still refuse, leave immediately; something else will surely have influenced the Oracles.

Dra'noxia lies in the ninth realm, also known as Cyphia. The city is run by an empress known as Tæmî, one of the highest members of the Circle that controls all of Cyphia. She should welcome you, should you meet her, but *do not draw attention to yourselves. If she does not notice you, do not approach her. There are too many forces at work, which could potentially sway her.*

Do not take your time in Cyphia. Speed is essential at this time. You must then travel to Vantrörkî to do what you can to heal the walls, else the realm will collapse. Remember, Vantrörkî is the shadow of all realms. Should it fall, all other realms will follow fast and the Void will be no welcome place. You should have around three months to reach the shadows, but try and be there at least a month beforehand, for travelling there will become increasingly difficult as the Gates are always the first to fall. Call our 'friend' if the need arises, and I feel he is right. You will need him to pass through Vantrörkî safely.

From there, there is little more I can tell you to do. You will know when you are needed and I feel your tasks will carry you through many realms, known and unknown. Both of you are truly ready for this task, even if you do not feel so at present. It is your destiny. I do not know what needs will come to light in your future; that is for you to know in time. Your decisions will light the way to safety.

In my desk, in the hidden drawer, I have kept Lee's prophecy. If the band is kept around the pages, it is feather-light and will take up next to no room in your packs. Take it with you, but do not read it. Prophecies should not be read by those they concern for many complications arise if they are. On the other hand, you are not to let others read it. People have a habit of repeating what they should not, or trying to manipulate another's destiny.

You will find many friends you will need in the near and far future, but also many friends who need you. Learn to distinguish them, for some of the latter will take you on paths you will not wish to take. They will no doubt use you for their own means, but as long as you all stay strong, your path will not be hampered by the like.

Camer, I understand if you choose to find your parents while on Vantrörkî, but in my heart and mind, you will ever remain my son. The Oathkeepers hold nothing over my soul, for it was not included in the terms, and so I will be with both of you always. Remember that and remember me.

I do have one request. Get one of the mages to preserve my body and if you get a chance, bring my daughters here. I may just be able to take a visible form near my body. They have a right to see me, whether I can or not. The ceremony must not go ahead until they have come here, for they too will have felt the loss, only they will not have understood it.

Finally, a few words of advice. Do not make Oaths on your soul, unless you wish to be a prisoner of the Oathkeepers forevermore. Nor should you make Oaths

Darkness

carelessly. Careless Oaths are the first to be broken - neither of you are to forget it.

Do not hold a grudge against the Oathkeepers, for they have one purpose in life, whether they like it or not. Indeed, they may need your help in the future and I expect you to be there to help them, despite what they are. Do not let me down because you are holding a grudge against them. It was never their fault. I knew they would come for me after all I have done. I am only surprised that they never came sooner.

Do not give your trust blindly, but do not totally ignore gut instinct. Some people are trustworthy and you will know them when you meet them.

Remain true to yourselves and stay on your path. Listen to others and note their advice, but never allow them to tell you what you must do. You are free to make your own choices. It is only through maintaining that freedom do you stand a chance of success.

No matter how it may have seemed, I am genuinely proud of you and you will always fill my thoughts wherever I come to rest.

And so I must end this last letter with all the love a father can give his sons.

Ever watching over you.

Scarien.

Mattias reread this letter several times, only he could

not take in the words. They were like a dot-art picture; always out of focus unless the eye found the pattern and concentrated solely on their meaning.

After about the fifteenth time, he shook his head and glanced at Camer. *He has every right to read this.* he thought, setting it on the table in front of his friend. He then walked over to the desk and located the drawer, hidden in the elaborate pattern. Sliding it open, he pulled out the prophecy and transferred it to the bottom of his pack. Sure enough, he could still get everything else on top of it and the pack was no heavier. Having completed that task, he glanced at his companion who was still staring blankly.

There was a soft but urgent knock at the door and Lyana made to open it. Remembering herself, she looked at Mattias, who nodded and made a small gesture to tell her to continue. She pulled it open quickly, a crack of light escaping from the room. Stepping aside, she allowed the two men to enter the office.

'Pardon the intrusion, sir, but-' began the taller of the two.

Mattias held up a hand, cutting across him, ignoring his own discomfort at giving so cold an order. Not looking at the men directly, and so hiding the true extent of his grief, he said, 'Firstly, do not call me sir. My name is

Mattias and I would rather be called by it.' The two men nodded and he continued to ask, 'What do you know of the Äescardïonas? Of the Oathkeepers?' he added at the man's confusion.

The man who had spoken blanched suddenly, as if someone had instantly drained him of all his blood. The other looked away, unwilling to speak.

'The … the…?' the first man stammered.

'Yes. You know of them, do you not? Tell me what you know of the Oathkeepers.' Mattias ordered, the words strange in his mouth, as if Scarien had spoken them.

The silent man looked at the youth, noticing the voice. In him, he saw Scarien, and instantly knew. The similarities were apparent: the way he stood, firm and strong whether he felt that way or not; his face, and more importantly the expression upon it - so fiery, yet able to soften suddenly; his voice, ringing through the air with a pure note to it, with enough force to halt an attacking army; and especially the eyes, which held the same depth and mystery, which also held in them a startling power, unexpected and dangerous.

He cleared his throat and Mattias looked at him briefly. 'Normally, I would keep my silence on such a topic for the Oathkeepers are not lightly spoken of. Though I made no Oath myself, sometimes silence with ignorance is better than the truth, for people tend to hold the truth against you. However, if Scarien's son commands it, I find myself ready to tell all I know.'

Mattias looked at him. 'How did you know?'

'You will never know how like him you are. Though he is no longer among us, he lives on through you. Everything I ever knew about him is standing in front of me.' Mattias felt his eyes burn and he looked determinedly at his feet. 'Anyway, what do you wish to know about the Äcscardïonas?'

Mattias shrugged, unable to think of any specifics. 'All you know would be a good start, I guess.'

The man paused. 'It is a long list of things in that case, with a tale behind it,' and he only continued once Mattias was seated comfortably and had indicated that he was ready. 'The Äescardïonas have forever lived in Äedescár. Although many theories have been established to contradict this. Some say that they were summoned by a mad god to punish his subjects. Others … well, they have less pleasant stories.

Everyone, or almost everyone I should say, comes to the same conclusion about their nature. On the whole, all other races believe them to be evil, but understandably, the

Äescardïonas themselves do not support this view. They may look, and act, the part, but in reality they are far beyond the terms good and evil. Those who escaped their realm described them as the Dystopia within Utopia, but they are beyond even that description. Indeed, they are indescribable in any of the tongues of the twelve habitable realms, for our words do them no justice.

'They do, however, have a name for themselves in their own language. In Äescar, their only language, they call themselves *Ha'sien umpachré Tro'naxer vox Nomin'xø* and nothing else.'

The sound that had passed his lips as he spoke those words was so similar to the voices of the Oathkeepers that Mattias could not suppress an involuntary shudder. But the soldier continued regardless, as if he had not noticed.

'We have no translation for it, but *Nomin'xø* can be interpreted as 'children' and altogether, we believe it loosely translates to 'Children of Balance', though *Ha'sien umpachré Tro'naxer* may also mean other things when split up. Some argue that they therefore have a religion and that they believe they were created by this balance. Personally, I do not agree with the idea, for they have no practices and few beliefs of any kind. If the Äescardïonas believe something, it is most likely to be fact.'

Mattias tried to interrupt at this point, but thought better of it and settled back in his chair, listening intently. *How can he know that?* he thought.

'They live cursed lives, which last for an eternity. They do not age, yet age dramatically at the same time, giving them the appearance of young and old simultaneously. They are ever bound to their one purpose in life, which happens also to be their only source of nourishment. It has been their only belief for many ages that their freedom will soon come. That appears to be their only desire: to be free from the pain they cause and the lives they live. To be given the chance to die of old-age or other natural causes is a fading dream.

'The Oaths people make are all they need to survive, for a broken Oath provides a limited resource of energy. An Oath that is kept, however, sustains them for as long as the Oath remains kept. Even through death an Oath can be broken, and so they sometimes find nourishment in Oaths that are millennia old. An Oath sworn on a soul leaves the victim as a slave for eternity if broken. If sworn on a life, the person is then free.

'Of course, some strong souls with good reason to break an Oath can be given a trial. Usually, their case is lost and they return to drift, or come to rest. Some have, however, been successful and their sentences overturned under certain conditions. They are then charged with a new Oath, which must never be broken, or their souls will be consumed.

'Äedescár is their homeland, and it really is a paradise beyond imagination. There is no black mark on the landscape, no imperfections. The people themselves are pleasant enough if you keep an Oath. The only people the Oathkeepers hate are those who refuse altogether to make an Oath, for it is those who deprive them of their only sustenance. They do not have much of a personality, although the children are as lively as any child of any race.

'They are immortal, unless blade or poison take them; they cannot heal as we do and are thus vulnerable, but they were not always so. They have tales of a life before, when their race was free to grow and develop like all others. They cannot freely reproduce, but when one dies, another is born and raised to sustain their population. There are so few of them that they cannot afford to fight amongst themselves, making them the most peaceful of all races, including the Clorans, who, in their time, had their own disagreements. They have no words for rage, anger, hate, war or the suchlike. Once the word exists, so does the thing that word represents. They do understand the words, however, having seen the reality in other realms.' He paused and cleared his throat.

Mattias stood and got him a glass of water, which he drank from gratefully.

'Please, continue.' said Lyana, unexpectedly, sitting on a small stool.

'It *is* true that they tortured the settlers from long ago, but they were fearful of what could come after. They are the only race not intended for war ... the only race since the Clorans passed on. The settlers would bring such problems with them. As well as this, they would bring currency and new customs, neither of which the Oathkeepers see need for.

'At the present time, there are ... *mutual friendships* between the peoples of the realms and the Oathkeepers.' He sounded as if he were choosing his words with great care and put great stress on 'mutual friendships' as if he did not agree with the term. 'Their emotions are subtle, and extraordinarily hard to read, but the signs become clearer with time. I must admit to having acquaintances among one particular team.

'Each team has eleven adults, and there are roughly one hundred teams. Plus two hundred children, making their population roughly thirteen hundred.'

Darkness

Mattias gave a gasp of surprise and shock. *So many...*

The soldier hastily continued. 'The number seems large, but not compared to the two billion Catréans, of the eight billion Humans, the two largest populations we know of. They are a small but highly significant race and represent, to a certain degree, the measures some turn to, to gain the trust of others. They are, all in all, the living proof that our actions have consequence, and we cannot escape it,' he stopped, choosing not to continue with his tale. Any more would be a great betrayal of information which was never meant for the outside world.

Mattias sensed his reluctance to continue and looked at Lyana, who had taken it upon herself to make a few notes. She nodded and handed him the notepad with her neat writing on it.

He stowed the pad away and turned his gaze to the soldiers. 'Now, what was it you wanted?' he asked.

The first man cleared his throat, the colour having returned to his face. 'Two things. Firstly, the Kha'sandric have attacked the training team to the north. All made it back alive with new co-ordinates,' and he handed Mattias a scrap of paper with a series of numbers hastily scribbled across it. 'And secondly, I have been informed that the Zyron tournaments have ended and the Zyrons themselves seem to be preparing for something once again. We presume an attack. Our correspondent will maintain his position and continue to deliver information.'

Mattias nodded. 'Thank you. Lyana, my second-in-command, will be in charge of this place in my absence. I must ask that my father's body be preserved in its present state. I know any of the mages can handle the task so please see to it ... either until he reawakens, if that happens, or at least until his daughters have seen him. It was his last wish and I intend to honour it.'

The men nodded and left as Mattias dismissed them. They would do anything to honour any dead man's last wish, especially their leader's, and so hurried to the Tower of the Dead, not forgetting to find a mage on their way up there.

Note to readers:

While mages in the common tongue are any who wield magick, in the realms where all can perform some sort of magick, determined by their race, mages would be far too common for it to be used as some form of title.

No, mages are much more special than one who can use magick. The mages are the only people of the realms to use certain magicks. These magicks are very rare and difficult to accomplish; it takes them many years of training and discipline to even be able to attempt such workings. These magicks include the ability to slow time and the ability to restore the soul. There are several others, all of which would normally require so much energy that it would kill the wielder.

Mages can work these spells and not even be fatigued. There is evidence that a gene mutation increases the likelihood of one reaching mage status.

The Clorans, however, can never be called mages. They are the ones who create magick that can be used, including the mages' spells. As a result, the Clorans are not restricted and the majority can use most magicks, although they will specialise in one or another.

To resume:

Lyana looked at Mattias. 'You still intend to leave?' she asked, slightly incredulous.

Mattias nodded. 'It's what he wanted. We have to go. He left some instructions … what he would have said.'

Camer moved for the first time since entering the office. He slowly looked at Mattias, his face still impassive but his eyes resigned. Carefully, he picked up the paper in front of his and began to read slowly. As he did so, Mattias handed Lyana the co-ordinates and she pocketed them.

Once Camer was finished, he held the letter out to Mattias, who folded it carefully and replaced it in its envelope, and then in his pocket. The boys then stood up together, Lyana following their lead.

'Nothing I can say to stop you?' she asked hopefully.

Mattias shook his head firmly and the three of them left the office and locked it. Mattias took the small key and hung it from the chain bearing the snake-pendant. He then drew a series of fiery symbols on the door, which blazed brightly for a few seconds before disappearing, leaving the wood unmarked.

'No one enters that room,' he said bluntly.

Lyana nodded and led the boys outside. The night air was chilly and she shivered as she left the warmth of the building.

'Do you have all you need?' she asked, knowing there was no point in trying to dissuade them now and she was not going to waste her breath on an already lost argument.

The boys nodded silently and Mattias began to open a Gate.

Lyana stepped back and began to walk away. 'Good luck and take care. Until we meet again, I guess,' she said briefly, before the night swallowed her fading form.

Mattias shot a concerned look at Camer, who just stood there. 'Now would be a good time Camer,' he said, not unkindly, but a touch of impatience entered his voice, unbidden. He opened the Gate wide enough for them to step through.

Camer looked at him, his eyes distant. Slowly, he stepped through, Mattias following close behind.

Behind them, the door wreathed in flames disappeared, leaving no trace of its being. As the Gate closed, so did that particular chapter in the boys' lives. It would linger only through memory.

The children are moving.
    Closer.
    Closer.

    Is that what I need?
    One.
    One will suffice.

Chapter 4

The Web of Magick

The eight champions said their farewells to Dracör and left the training halls silently, their conversation currently exhausted. As they walked out into the street, however, they heard a shout. Stopping to look around, they saw a village guard running towards them, signalling to his colleague as he passed him.

'Qwenox, you are required to stand before the Council urgently. We have been sent to escort you,' he panted, out of breath.

His partner ran up behind him, stopping short. *~Good. You've found them,~* he said, looking as if he had been searching all day.

He glanced behind him as the seventeenth bell was rung. Directing his words at the children, he said, *~We've been looking everywhere for you. Now come on, and don't* *wander off. You should not have disappeared earlier after the tournament,~* and he led them through the streets, his co-worker bringing up the rear, making sure none of them strayed from the group and off into the rest of the village. They did not want another search for them.

Even though Caya was used to the buildings changing every time they were approached, she could not help but stop and stare at the Council Halls; the building was a deep sapphire blue and the stone naturally patterned in a way that caught and held the eye, making it dance trying to follow a single line. The pattern rippled and changed, and every time she tried to find one part, her gaze was drawn to another.

Within mere moments she was lost in the intricate design, her mind focussed solely on the stone. Her subconscious self managed to briefly remember what Xanor had said not an hour before, about the Citadel of Tresh. It was the same stone, the same enchantment. But her mind could not, nor had any desire to, break free.

Qyan stepped in front of her, blocking her view to no avail. He put his hands on her shoulders and shook her gently, staring into her eyes for a response. The blankness remained, like two empty holes instead of eyes. Her mind had become detached from her body and could not find its

Darkness

way back, lost in the web. Qyan separated his own mind from his natural boundaries to search for her, and the final ring of the seventeenth bell echoed like a death bell.

*　*　*　*　*　*　*　*　*　*　*　*

He searches, moving quickly. Initially, he searches the immediately surrounding area, but soon moves to search the whole village. He soon realises that she is nowhere to be found in open air. The only place left to search is within the stone itself.

Cautiously, he approaches the stone, ignoring the eye-catching patterns. He absently notices the pealing vibrations of the eighteenth bell as the sound rings through him. He wonders if he really has been 'out' for so long. But he dismisses the fact and focuses on the task in hand, not allowing himself to get distracted. Distractions take up even more time.

He sends a tendril of thought to the stone. He is not even faintly surprised when he finds it not to be stone. It is a magickal construct formed by the Clorans from raw, wild magick. It was still wild inside. Nothing could tame it. None other than the Clorans had the ability or the power of craft. He recognises the enchantment that Xanor had told them of. He knows the risks. But in this state, he is not being drawn in. It holds no power over him like this.

Determining it to be safe for him to proceed, he enters the construct, the web of magick enclosing him as a spider would a fly that is caught in its web. Indeed, he feels like a fly, weaving through, trying not to get tangled in the strands of magick. If he does, he, too, will be trapped. As he moves, he continually feels as if the spider has its eyes on him, its prey to be.

Instantly his world is transformed. He cannot help but examine the structure, its bizarre complexity. He realises quickly that few could ever have created it as the builders would need to be skilled in all elements - including the main four - as well as magickal construction at the same time. Even among the Clorans, when they were around, few would have the skill. It was a talent of the Elders. No Elementalist can match such a feat.

As he searches for Caya, he finds flaws in the web; holes that need to be repaired. The construct is deteriorating and the Elementalists can never repair it, despite the fact the wild magick may break free. The holes help him navigate through the spell, but one wrong move can bring the whole thing down around him, destroying anything inside. Moving swiftly, but with more care, he spies Caya nestled in the web, peaceful yet trapped. Glancing around, he sees several other consciousnesses, all trapped, all as if asleep.

He moves carefully so as not to get caught himself, and even more carefully as he detangles his friend, aware that a false or hasty move could destroy the construct along with all caught inside. It is like disarming a bomb without letting it explode, and with a crowd of people gathered around him. He has control over their lives now. They are all depending on him.

Once Caya is free, she is instantly alert, the spell releasing her from her slumber. A faint sound passes through the stone, but he ignores it, focussed on his team-mate.

~Where am I?~ she asks, fear setting in.

Qyan moves quickly, holding her still. Softly, he speaks, calming her. ~Inside the stone. Come, we must free the others.~ *He frowns slightly, feeling something strange.* ~We do not have much time. Move quickly and help me. But be careful. You do not want to get trapped again and this construct is deteriorating. Move with caution.~

They work quickly, freeing all the souls held prisoner in the spell. Some become aware of their surroundings within seconds. For others, it takes much longer, or not at all. Those who remain in their sleep-like state are led out by those unable to otherwise help. The more alert and careful aid the children, working as quickly as possible to free their fellow prisoners.

Many hours pass, but eventually the task seems near completion. The last few minds are carefully untangled and leave the stone.

To be completely sure, Qyan leads a small team of the more alert minds to search for any others trapped in the web but they find no more. Breathing a mental sigh of relief that nothing nasty had happened and that the feeling of being watched is in his mind, Qyan and the group return to the outside air where the others are waiting, unsure of where their bodies are. They surround Qyan, their thoughts questioning, fearful.

Quickly, he tries to contact one of the other team members, but fails. He is surprised that they are still waiting here. Surely they would have moved them by now.

~Caya, could you return and ask where I should take all these we have rescued. We need to get them settled before they panic.~

She does so quickly and he watches as her body begins to move. He waits for the vibrations of her voice, and when they come, they are clear and easy for him to comprehend.

'Those lost in the stone, where are their bodies?' Caya asks the guards, the sound pure. 'They need to be returned quickly.'

The guards mumble something to each other, clearly uncomfortable, muffling the vibrations. After a few moments, Qyan begins to understand some of their talk.

'What should we say?' asks one to the other.

'Nothing. We are not permitted to speak of the events surrounding the stone. You go and find the high-councillors and ask them to come; only they can say.'

'But what if the boy has found them? Surely they would need to return soon. You know the connection deteriorates once they leave that thing. Remember the one who broke free last summer. He was fine until he was out of the stone.'

Darkness

'It's too unlikely. Many have searched, and he is just a child. Now go.'

The guard runs into the building without any more questions, the other waiting outside to watch the children, looking impatient. No one, Qyan notices, is looking at the stone, their fear of it as clear as Caya's voice.

The guard returns after only a few minutes, followed closely by Jared who immediately dismisses them.

'Where is he Caya?' Jared asks.

Caya casts a meaningful glance at the air above them. 'We found the rest. They're all out we think.'

Jared does not reply, but instead directs his thoughts at Qyan.

~Qyan. Their bodies are in the House of Healing. The top floor. You will need to make sure they enter the correct bodies for their connections will have deteriorated too much for them to merely float into them. Some may remember where to go, but those still lethargic will need help.~

~The restricted level? I did wonder what happened up there,~ *Qyan mused.*

~Yes. Before you go, what bell did you leave on?~ *Jared asks urgently.*

~The seventeenth. Why?~

Jared represses his anguish. ~Do you know what time it

99

is? You have been out too long. Hurry!~

Qyan lingers still. ~But why?~

~I'll explain later. When you're back. Now go. Don't take too long. We'll meet you there.~

Qyan envelopes those unwilling to go and, with the help of those eager to return to their physical forms, he takes them to the House of Healing, dimly registering the strain on his mind.

They get there quickly, though they may have made the journey quicker had they been in their best condition. Qyan analyses each mind and directs each to the corresponding body. With a little help, the still sleeping are settled into their respective bodies before the helpers return to their own, thanking Qyan as they go.

Qyan watches as some begin to stir, awaking after a long separation before entering a healing sleep. He feels mental exhaustion setting in and thinks he can ignore it for a few hours longer.

He leaves the House of Healing in search of his body, unwilling to wait for Jared. The connection is growing fainter, making it hard to navigate accurately. His growing tiredness obscures his ability to search properly.

After a couple of hours, he realises he should have waited. Returning to the House of Healing he begins to drift, finding it harder to stay alert and whole.

~Qyan. Where are you?~ *calls Caya. He makes for the*

sound, unable to reply.

After what feels like eternity, he begins to drift once more. He has barely the strength to remain whole. He knows he should try to return, but the thought strays almost as soon as it is formed. He hears the others calling him, but cannot make out their words.

Another mind suddenly envelopes him, preventing him from falling apart. He has not the strength to fight back and feels himself being carried by the other consciousness. He lets himself be taken, unable to resist.

In a short while, he finds himself being pushed into a body. His body. Relief surges through him as he settles into the restrictions; the physical chains restraining him once more. He is safe and can now sleep.

* * * * * * * * * * * *

Jared paced back and forth through the room. In the street below, people made their way home for the evening, ready for a meal and sleep; all were oblivious of the problem above their heads. Beyond the mountain, it was night once more. Nearly twenty-one hours had passed since Qyan had left. That combined with his constant working had almost severed the link with his body.

Note to readers:

There is a lot here that really should be explained, and I haven't really had a moment before now to do so.

First of all, the stone is not true stone. Cloric is a realm, sustained by the wild magick that fills it from the Void. This wild magick spontaneously creates a liquid which runs underground, like rivers, constantly being renewed. The Clorans managed to bring some of it to the surface for their own use.

They soon discovered, that while they could not change the substance, they could create hardened structures from it. These small creations had such intricate patterns which would capture the eye. Intrigued by these, the Clorans set about rebuilding their realm.

They found three varieties of the Ora: white, red and blue. They built up their cities with the white form, the patterns hidden more by the colour, therefore lessening the effect. This allowed them to be near its beauty on a daily basis. The Citadel of Tresh, however, needed the strongest form; the deep, sapphire blue. It was the rarest of the three and by far the most beautiful. The remaining citadels were built using the red variety.

This brilliant Ora is purely wild magick and while it can be shaped, it could never be tamed. Raw magick has a need for sustenance. It uses the minds of others to take new forms and to grow and change.

The patterns are so enticing, they literally steal your mind.

Secondly, when one's mind is detached from the body, there are certain strands which serve as an anchor. The longer you spend away from your body, the weaker these strands become, eventually breaking altogether. Should the connections break, the mind will not recognise its body as its own. They can go without ever being connected again, the body eventually dying and the mind drifting apart, becoming fragments in the world around.

The Ora traps the mind, keeping it in a slumber-like state. This stops the connection from breaking, as it is the activity that weakens the bonds.

Any questions?

To resume:

Caya shook her head to clear the post-separation dizziness. She walked towards Jared, who turned to face her, his face lined with worry.

~*Well?*~ he asked anxiously.

~*He's back,*~ she replied, smiling at him before moving towards the bed on which Qyan lay.

Qyan was still unmoving, though there had been slight twitching as his mind rejoined his body. His face was unnaturally white and ice-cold to the touch. The team was gathered around the bed, waiting for their team-mate to reawaken.

Jared approached slowly and they stepped aside to let him through. He sat on the bed and laid a hand on the side of the boy's face.

~*Xanor, could you find Healer Samîstra? Tell her I sent you,*~ he said quickly.

He watched as Xanor ran out of the room before returning his gaze and attention to the unconscious youth.

~*Come on Qyan,*~ he said. ~*I know you're in there. You can make it. Come on.*~

Xanor returned a few minutes later, a young Healer hot on his heels. Jared stood and stepped back to allow her room. She immediately swept down to examine her latest charge.

For several tense moments, the others watched worriedly until she withdrew.

~*He should be fine. How long was he out?*~ she asked gently.

Jared began to reply, but Iano cut across him. ~*Since the seventeenth bell yesterday. He was out overnight. It took several hours to detangle only a few minds from the enchantment's web. With so many, it took far too long. Even with some help from those he had freed.*~

Samîstra turned to him. ~*He was inside the stone?*~

The whole team nodded and looked at the bed. Qyan stirred slightly, like a sleeper lost in his dreams. He did not awaken, but slept on. However, some colour made its way back into his complexion, giving him a slightly healthier look.

Samîstra shook her head. *~From careful monitoring of those the stone had captured, we found that somehow, the magick enabled them to maintain a connection to their body for extremely long periods of time … months, some even years. This boy must have been outside the stone for longer than he was in it. Only a few hours would have caused severe damage. But he is strong.~* She smiled reassuringly. *~His mind has settled well. He should be up and about tomorrow. The young always heal quickly.~*

Deciding to call it a day, the majority of Qwenox made to take their leave. They were feeling the strain of having been up since the previous day's morning, and wanted to go to bed. They had not rested since the draining effects of using their magick in battle.

~Are you coming Caya?~ Xanor asked when she didn't move with them.

~In a minute. Go ahead. I'll catch you up,~ she said softly, smiling slightly.

The boy nodded and took his leave with the rest of the team, heading to bed for a good night's sleep.

~Are you going to be okay here?~ Jared asked Caya, sensing her intention.

~Of course. Why wouldn't I be? I can sleep quite happily here. Anyway, what was it you wanted earlier ... yesterday even?~

~It can wait for now. I'll find you later.~ Jared replied with a smile. After a brief pause, he left, leaving Caya on her own.

She located a chair and pulled it up to the side of the bed. Sitting in it, she found it rather comfortable. Healer Samîstra was back, and she listened to the Healer moving about the room, not seeing her casting approving looks to the corner where the bed was situated.

After a while, she came over with a blanket, somehow aware of Caya's plans to stay the night. Handing it over, she said, ~It can get very cold in here at night. If there's anything else I can get you, just shout.~

Caya smiled and thanked her, accepting the blanket gratefully. While she unfolded it, the healer left; she had other more urgent problems to deal with. Caya curled up cat-like in the chair and tucked the blanket around herself, falling asleep almost instantly.

* * * * * * * * * * *

Qyan awoke to the silence of the ward. He felt oddly dizzy and was, to begin with, at a loss as to where he

Darkness

actually was. Looking to his left, he saw Caya asleep on a chair, a blanket that may have initially covered her hanging from the chair, held only by her hand resting on it.

He tried to push himself up, but fell back again, his arms unable to take the weight. The movement, however, succeeded in awakening the sleeping girl. Qyan looked at her apologetically as she blinked the sleep from her eyes.

~*Hello stranger,*~ she smiled, stretching out a bit to work the stiffness from her limbs. ~*How are you?*~

He looked back at her, a hint of a smile playing about his lips. ~*Hello yourself. I feel a bit weak, but that will probably pass with time. At least, I hope it will.*~

She studied his face for a moment, noting how tired and drawn out he looked, despite the fact he had slept the night soundly. It worried her to see him in this condition, but instead of commenting, however, she concentrated on helping him sit up, moving the pillows to support him.

The Healer walked in and saw him sitting up, awake. ~*Good. Now that you're awake, could you give me a minute to sort myself out? I need to talk to you.*~

Qyan and Caya waited patiently as she went back and forth about the room, preparing it for a transfer and other possible patients. She worked quickly and soon walked over to the corner, clipboard in hand. She immediately began running a series of tests to determine

Qyan's condition at that time.

~Right,~ she said, finally finished. ~I think you should be able to leave any time after the fourteenth bell, and not a second before. You're a very lucky young boy. As you've probably worked out for yourself, it is not a good idea to stay separated for hours at a time.

~Eventually, with much training, you may be able to achieve it, but it must be done in healthy stages. You might not be so lucky next time.~ She paused, making a few notes before continuing. ~The mind and body have a connection that is vital for the survival of both. That connection must be maintained at all times and staying separated for so long weakens it. Eventually, it is broken.~

She paused again, writing a few more notes on her clipboard. ~The stone somehow allows the connection to be maintained, so most of those you rescued are fine. We are running some therapies to help them become re-accustomed to their bodies.~ She smiled at him. ~I also advise you to rest for the next few days. No over-exertion for the next week or so. But that is simply what I would recommend. If you choose to ignore me, that's your problem.~ And with that cheerful note, she swept out of the room.

Caya stood up and retrieved the blanket from the floor, folding it carefully. ~I'm hungry. I'm going to find something to eat. I'll bring something up for you if you want.~

Qyan nodded. *~I'm starving. Anything will do.~*

Caya walked out in search of food and Qyan closed his eyes in thought. So much had happened. The more he thought about it, the more he wanted to leave with the girls. He felt some sort of need to stay with them.

A few minutes later, Jared entered the room quietly. Qyan opened his eyes at the slight sound and nodded to the high-councillor in greeting.

Jared smiled as he realised the boy was awake. *~Is the traveller feeling any better today?~*

Qyan shrugged. *~I could say that,~* he said briefly, still thinking about leaving the mountain.

Jared raised his eyebrows. *~Ask it. I'll answer to the best of my abilities. And don't deny you have a question.~*

If Qyan was in any way surprised that Jared knew he wished to ask him a question, he hid it extremely well; his face and voice remained as impassive as ever. *~When the girls leave to go to the Letrans, can we go with them? The team, I mean.~*

Jared thought about it for an agonising few seconds. *~I don't see why not. But may I ask why?~*

~I do not believe we would continue with tournaments anyway. The team would feel wrong without the girls. It makes more sense to stick together. We have grown close. We look out for each other.~

~I'll talk to Ganto, and the Council, on your behalf. But regardless of their decision, you may go if you want to. If anyone questions your departure refer them to me. It is your right to go where you will.~

Qyan nodded. *~Thank you.~*

~My pleasure. Now, I'm going to give you some advice for the world outside. Smile more. You are far too impassive all of the time and people find you harder to approach because of it. And when you do smile, the expression is unnaturally strange, but nicer ... friendlier. Beyond this mountain, people will not know you. Although impassiveness will cause them to keep their distance, it will make it much harder to communicate with them. They will be more unwilling to linger for conversation.~

Qyan nodded and closed his eyes, pensive.

~If it means anything more, I approve of you leaving for the Letrans. If I were free to make my own choices, I'd have left long before, along with many others. Remember that.~

~You are still young, you can make your choices now and you have the chance to make the right ones. While the Council still insists the Letrans are evil, I would say neither side is right or wrong. We are too held back, while they move forward too quickly. It is good for the young, but for us older people, change is too much to handle.~

Jared stopped suddenly as the door opened slowly. Caya walked in with a tray full of food, all balanced rather

Darkness

precariously. She did not seem surprised to see Jared in the room, but simply put the tray on the chair she had slept in and said, *~I wasn't sure what you wanted, so I got a bit of everything.~*

Qyan smiled faintly and nodded, pulling himself up properly to look at the food, while failing to hide his amusement. Locating a plate underneath the toast, he served himself some fruit and began to eat. The food he ate, though little, was satisfying and settled comfortably in his almost empty stomach. He sat back once he had finished, feeling slightly stronger than he had before.

* * * * * * * * * * * *

An hour before his being discharged, Qyan was walking about the ward. The healer had been to check on him several times over the course of the day and he was becoming bored of the same scenery. Apparently, deep meditation came under the heading 'over-exertion' and could prove unnecessary strain on the mind. As for detaching his mind and wandering; it was out of the question. Caya had left him earlier to find the rest of the team and had not yet returned.

As if his thoughts held some unknown summoning power, Caya walked in through the open door alone.

~I either keep missing them, or they've been summoned before the Council. I couldn't find them anywhere and no one could tell me where they are,~ she said and shrugged, sounding slightly irritated.

Qyan sat on the bed. *~Only half an hour to go. Then we can get out of this place. I cannot wait.~* He looked at her, his face as expressionless as ever. *~I never asked, and you never said, but what is it like beyond the mountain?~*

She walked over and sat next to him. *~You're thinking of coming with us, aren't you?~* she asked, already knowing the answer.

~I have already asked Jared, and he agrees that it would be a good idea. The whole team can come, if they want to.~

She sighed, but not out of irritation or resignation. Instead, it was more as if she missed the outside world and was bringing back fond memories. *~The realm outside the mountain. It's amazing ... beautiful. And noisy compared to here. In the towns, there are always the sounds of people talking as they move about the streets. Lots of conversation but the words are hard to make out. The words blend into each other and you have to really listen to concentrate on one voice. There is the occasional sound of a cart as it wheels past. The marketers shout out how much of a bargain their goods are. Dawn is preceded, accompanied and followed by the most amazing chorus from the birds. Throughout the day, they continue only with less volume.*

Darkness

At night, the town sleeps, as do most birds, but the night-creatures make their own sound to break the silence. Though it is never silent, it is often peaceful. If no animals make their noises, the wind whistles past you, or the rain plays a beat on the ground.

~Outside the towns are the expanses of countryside. There are the marked trails if you wish to journey along a scenic route, but some people go cross-country, ignoring all paths. It's not just green, as most people think. Amongst the many shades of green are yellows, reds, purples, blues and oranges all year round. In winter, the colours become crisp and are brushed with an icy white, while in summer the sun makes the colours all the brighter. Each shade appears to give off its own light. The light showers lay a mist over them in the early morning, but it always rises, making them seem even more vivid. The gold comes out in autumn; even the poorest can seem rich amongst it. With each season, the realm changes and each sight is unique, never to be seen again.

~Once, a Jumper told me that there are places even more beautiful, but I cannot imagine them.~

Qyan closed his eyes, picturing her words to the best of his ability. But having never witnessed such a thing before in his life, he could not see it all, large gaps appearing in the images, many of the colours grey and faded.

The Elementalists Series

The fourteenth bell rang and they quickly took their leave of the ward. As they left the building and stepped into the well-lit street, they walked, literally, into Jared. He looked incredibly worried and steered them straight to the Council Halls without saying a word, ignoring their repeated questions.

Once inside the building, he looked the two in the eyes, speaking quickly. *~You've been summoned, as you can guess, but I must tell you before you enter. Whatever you do, do not let them know that you know this. Your father Caya, Scarien Éscaronôvic, died. The Oathkeepers took him. We found out not long ago. The Elders are going to try and make you stay here. You mustn't let them. I'll do all I can, but it might be down to you. Come up with a story, anything.*

~Here's why I say this. Again, don't let them find out that you know, but Scortia, and the rest of Qwenox are missing. We've searched everywhere. They've gone. All of them. To find them, you must find Mattias, your brother. He and his friend, who fills Vyus's place, will help you.

~They need you also, to help repair a realm due to collapse. For that you need your sister. He will have much to tell you. Listen to what he says, it will be important. Help them. Help the Letrans. You must go to Dra'noxia. You will find Mattias there. He will-~

~Jared, bring them in.~ came a stranger's voice.

114

Darkness

~*Go. Now.*~ and Jared pushed the children through the double stone doors, following them in and shutting them inside.

Lost.

Trapped.

These worlds must be set free.

Confined.

Cut off.

The Void shall grow.

Existence will be reborn.

Chapter 5

The Meeting

Jared left them and took his seat by Ganto. All fourteen of the high-councillors were present as well as five Elders. All of them, bar Jared, bore grim expressions.

The room was large and circular. The Elders sat at the far side, in the centre of the group. The high-councillors sat seven on either side. Their throne-like chairs lined the edge of the circle, creating part of a semi-circle around a central platform. By the door, where the team-mates stood, were lines of seats with an aisle down the centre, seemingly in waiting for an audience.

~Approach,~ said the Elder seated in the centre. He was obviously the oldest of them all.

The youths nervously walked up to the Council and stepped onto the platform, facing them.

The man who had addressed them stood. After a brief pause, he spoke. *~The Council addresses Qyan Aguana and*

Caya Éscaronôvic of Water. Both have responded to a summons sent out today at the thirteenth stroke of the day.~ He paused again while a scribe in the corner wrote down what had been said. *~The Council recognises the death of one Scarien Éscaronôvic, a traitor, but a great Elementalist nonetheless. May the Elements guide him.~*

~May the Elements guide him,~ repeated the rest of the Council.

~Éscaronôvic was the recognised leader of the breakaway group the Letrans. Since they are no longer bound to the Oath, the two Children of Destiny *in our care are to remain here indefinitely.~*

~As prisoners?~ asked Caya, forgetting her manners accidentally-on-purpose.

One of the women next to the Elder who had spoken smiled strangely. *~No. As guests.~*

~Surely guests are free to leave as and when they wish,~ Qyan retorted. *~These guests have other places to be.~*

~That is correct.~ The smile slipped from the woman's face.

The man raised a hand for order and continued, *~They will remain here indefinitely to train as a Zyron. That is all. You are dismissed.~* And she sat down.

~I don't want to stay here!~ Caya said angrily. *~I want to go home. See my friends. Breathe fresh air again.~*

~What you want and what you get are two completely different things Miss Éscaronôvic. The Elders have spoken. You stay here whether you like it or not. Do not disrupt the way of the Zyrons,~ said one of the high-councillors, half-standing.

Jared stood and spoke 'privately' with the Council, slyly allowing Qyan and Caya to hear the conversation. *~Surely force will achieve nothing. The prophecy was very clear with what would happen to those who forced the will of the Children. Only their free choices could bring a favourable outcome. Forcing them will lead to our ruin.~*

~Jared does have a point,~ a young woman mused. *~We are not to force their hand if we wish to come out better. If she wishes to leave, let her.~*

~Thank you Sifi.~

~No need Jared, I know the truth when it's in front of me.~

The Council broke out into deep argument, little of it making sense to the children. Within only a few minutes, almost everyone was on their feet, shouting about something or another. Accusations swung back and forth and insults flew freely. The Elders talked amongst themselves, remaining seated, ignoring the chaos in the room.

~What if she finds out about the other?~ the Elder asked, the other Elders nodding in agreement. Everyone quietened rapidly.

~She won't,~ said Jared. ~We can say she has gone on ahead.~

~But she will then question why we wished her to remain.~

Jared seemed to be thinking hard. ~We were testing her will. This mountain needs protection and we would of appreciated her staying. Like her sister, she's strong-willed.~

There was a general murmur of assent as everyone took their seats again, some somewhat grudgingly.

With the Council settled, the Elder addressed the teens again. ~Very well. Go where you will. I have nothing more to say on the matter. Jared will escort you, since he seems to know best on this matter.~ And he left with the air of a powerful person suddenly humbled.

Jared stood again and led the two outside. ~That's that settled. It's high time he was overruled, the pompous good-for-nothing scumbag. Stuck in the past, the lot of them. I hate Elders. It can be so tiring to change their mind, manipulating their views for the better. Be thankful you are leaving.~

Caya smiled. ~Before we go, you'll need to show us how to open a Gate.~

Jared nodded, leading them to the training halls. He pulled them inside one of the rooms that had always been locked.

~Normally, entry is only permitted once a person is

twenty-five years of age. To prying children, the door remains barred. That rule is only being broken today so we are not disturbed, and because this is one of the few rooms that are properly sound-proofed. A Gate is incredibly loud, unless the opener has enough experience to weave in a silencing spell.~ He smiled. *~When an Elementalist opens a Gate, it represents the element they belong to – Fire, Water, Earth or Air. Different races and groups within races have distinguished Gates. On top of that, every Gate is unique to the individual, displaying part of their character.~*

He drew several symbols in the air, each remaining etched there as if he had carved into wood, each sign shining a brilliant blue. After the fifth, he flicked his wrist and they grew and stretched until they formed an arch.

~These symbols are for all Gates, no matter the destination. They make up the physical part of it. The rest is done solely with the mind. It is important to focus on your destination, either by name or feature. Otherwise, the Gate will not open in the right place. Also, the door cannot be opened physically. You must visualise it opening and make it so.~ He demonstrated, the arch shining brightly for a moment before opening slowly, a shaft of light appearing as if a door really was opening.

As the shaft filled the Gate, the children found that they could not see what lay beyond. There was only the light. They looked to Jared for guidance and the Elder nodded them through.

They did so, cautiously, seeming to come out instantly on the far side. They found themselves at the top of a small hill, with broken countryside as far as they could see. Across the expanse, cities and towns could be seen scattered about, marring what would otherwise be perfect greenery. Jared stepped through behind them, closing the Gate and shutting out the deafening sound.

~*If you are unspecific when selecting your destination, for example, if you just think of a realm or a rough area within a realm, the Gate will open in a secluded spot, designed specifically for the opening of Gates. If you are more specific however,*~ He opened another Gate and stepped through into the space behind them. ~*then you go where you specifically choose to.*~

Caya spoke as the Gate closed, cutting out the sound. ~*Why is it so noisy?*~ she asked curiously.

~*No one knows. Always shut a Gate behind you unless you are going straight back through. It minimises the disturbance to the realm walls. This is the silencing symbol. Only use it when necessary. It is rather draining to attempt.*~ He handed Caya a small piece of paper with a symbol drawn on it. Memorising it, she passed it to Qyan, who nodded once before handing it back to Jared.

~*There's nothing else I can do for you, except to wish you*

Darkness

luck.~

He stepped back and nodded to the pair. Caya smiled before drawing and opening a Gate.

~Thank you,~ she murmured as she stepped through.

Qyan simply nodded again before following her. There was nothing left to say.

Jared watched as the Gate closed before returning to the Council Halls. What they did next was up to them. He could interfere no more.

* * * * * * * * * * * *

Two days after arriving on Cyphia, Camer had started to recover from the grief. Having something else to do and think about kept his mind too busy to return to that night and the horrors it held. Mattias, on the other hand, had found some hidden reserves of strength to lean on and found himself coping remarkably well, all things considered.

Dra'noxia was a large city and was one that never slept. At all hours of the day there were pockets of activity, lighting up the place and giving it life. All of Cyphia itself was permanently bathed in the soft golden glow of the three suns. The suns sometimes rotated in position, but they never sank or heightened in the cloudless sky. At first, the boys found that this warm light lifted their spirits and broke through the darkness they felt. As their first day wore on, however, they found themselves cursing the sunlight, longing for night to fall so that they could rest in comfort.

In the streets, everyone moved around freely, not restricted by any customs of the realm. Out-realmers were just another part of society and so the boys felt no need to try and fit in. No one spared them a second glance. Also, the rushed atmosphere and the fact everyone hurried everywhere, allowed them to move in haste without looking conspicuous for having no other means of transport.

The two were currently sitting on a hill, eating a quick lunch. From here they could see the city from above, watching the specks that were people rush back and forth. They had found the Destiny Halls the previous day, but as of yet, they had not found a way inside. The great square-ish building was impenetrable. Camer had examined the wall structure several times, confused. It was some kind of mineral he had not yet encountered, but it was strong. Stronger than diamond. There were no windows, no doorways, and as far as he could tell, no way in.

And so they had taken their time exploring the city.

Darkness

They had been in and out of various shops, gazing curiously and the remarkable items to be found, apparently from all realms.

Mattias finished his meal before Camer. It was a nice walk into the hills and there was still much more exploring they wished to do. They had been trying to work out how time ran on Cyphia, for to them, the days were uncannily irregular. They had already spent a lot of time looking at clocks and watches that all carried different symbols around the edge and different intervals, and all of which moved at various differing speeds. It was as if each individual worked to their own time in whatever way they pleased.

Packing away the last of their lunch, they continued their trek. They were aiming to reach the visitors' centre before nightfall on Catré, using Mattias's watch to keep some sort of time. If they could not get there in time they planned to spend yet another 'night' camping in one of the caves that littered the slopes around the city.

They had only been walking for about an hour by Mattias's reckoning when they heard the sound of a Gate opening nearby. Camer's fists clenched, recognising the sound that brought the Oathkeepers to Scarien. Mattias lay a hand on his friend's shoulder in warning. Looking down into the valley, they saw the Gate, two people emerging from it.

~Wait. It's my sister,~ Mattias murmured, sensing their connection immediately.

Carefully, the boys edged closer, using one of the hidden routes they had found previously. Once on the same level, Mattias conjured a fireball, keeping it hidden in his palm, just in case. After all, he had no clue as to the other's identity.

Qyan stiffened, feeling the pair approach. Silently, he alerted Caya, sharing his concerns. He could not sense their intentions and it worried him.

Caya nodded slightly, sitting down in the grass. Qyan was already tiring quickly, and so followed suit, grateful for the opportunity to rest. However, he remained alert, unsure of the strangers. Caya smiled and handed him a water bottle, telling him to drink.

~One is my brother. I can feel his presence. It feels different to any other. Warm, burning...~ she said while he drank. ~I don't think we have anything to fear from them.~

~Be prepared. Just in case your feeling is wrong,~ he replied, using some of his waning strength to reply telepathically.

~You need to sleep. I'll keep watch while you rest, Qyan,~ she instructed, removing her pack so that he could use it as some sort of pillow.

As he drifted into the uncharted realm of sleep, Caya stood up to get a glimpse of the two boys. They were just standing there, staring down towards her. One held a ball of flames and both were tense; yet she could not tell whether they were going to attack or were merely being cautious.

She drew her sword, a parting gift from Jared. It was a small, light blade, but flawless in every way. In a similar way to the sword Senti carried, it alerted her to various dangers. Slowly, she lay it down on the ground in front of her before doing the same with her bow and arrows.

She watched apprehensively as the boys mimicked the gesture, their multitude of weapons disturbing her. But the meaning of the action was clear, and after a brief moment, they all picked up their equipment and replaced them in their appropriate places.

Mattias and Camer shared a quick glance before making their way down towards Caya. The girl sat down once again, glancing briefly at her companion, making sure he was okay.

'Caya?' Mattias asked, also sitting down, making himself comfortable.

She nodded as Camer slung his pack from his back,

settling it on the ground. 'You're my brother, a Fire Elementalist?' she asked, the question rhetorical.

'Yes, I am,' Mattias replied, not picking up on the tone as his attention was on the sleeping Qyan. 'My companion is Camer, the replacement for Earth.' He turned his gaze back to Caya. 'Where is Scortia?'

Caya shrugged, trying to appear unconcerned. 'The rest of the team disappeared before we left. We are going to find them.' She turned to Camer. 'He is not our brother,' she stated simply.

'No. Vyus was killed before you and your sister were born. As the position of Earth must be filled, Camer takes his place as our father's adopted son.'

Caya looked intently at Camer's face, his expression completely blank. His eyes, however, were filled with sadness and confusion. She knew what had happened, or at least what she had been told had happened, but she wanted to be sure. His expression was all she needed, but she asked regardless. 'Is it true? Is he…?'

Mattias nodded silently, gently laying a hand on Camer's shoulder. He glanced down at Qyan, his eyes asking the question he refused to voice.

'This is Qyan Aguana. He is my team-mate and good friend. There are six others for you to meet, including

Scortia. We trained together and competed together. I was told that I would find them by finding you.'

Mattias shrugged. 'I don't know where they are. How should I? All I know is that we will need your sister for us to save a realm. If Vantrörkî is to collapse, all existence would fall with it.' He leaned against a rock behind him. 'What's wrong with him?' he asked, switching the subject back to Qyan.

'He was lost, but now he is found. A vital bond must be remade within,' she answered cryptically, saying no more.

Mattias almost made to ask what she meant, but thought better of it. Instead, he pulled out Scarien's letter and handed it to her. 'This was from our father. He would have wanted you to read it.'

Caya nodded, reading over the words quickly. *The words of a dead man. A dead man I never knew. Yet he can reach me so easily through a piece of paper,* she thought, taking in not only what was written, but the small detail of his handwriting. It was a script so uncannily similar to her own and the similarities were unsettling.

After a while, she folded the letter carefully, handing it back to Mattias, turning her attention to Qyan. 'He saved my life, and I his. I only hope he can now pull through this next battle,' she murmured, feeling the need to somewhat explain his presence.

Mattias nodded, unsure of what to say. Instead, an uncomfortable silence passed over the group. None of them moved, just sitting on the hill.

Camer turned, looking down towards the town. Slowly, panic filled him and he glanced at Mattias's watch. Jumping up, he grabbed his pack. 'Shift change!' he shouted, already off up the hill.

Mattias grabbed his things, swearing. 'Nearest cave?' he called after the retreating boy.

Camer paused only to reply. 'Five minutes away.'

Mattias shoved his stuff in place. 'Wake your friend,' he instructed Caya. 'Once we are safe, I'll explain everything. For now, just grab your things and run.' He took off after Qyan, glancing back to make sure she followed.

Caya frowned, waking Qyan. The boys' urgency had alarmed her and she slung her pack on her back as Qyan sat up, taking his as well.

Instantly alert to danger, Qyan stood, staggering after Mattias. Caya moved quickly to support her friend and together they made slow progress.

~*I cannot make it. Leave me here, Caya. I am only slowing you down,*~ he said, stopping. He could feel his mind

Darkness

already shutting down again, needing to rest further.

~No Qyan. Come on and quit complaining. This is no time to become a martyr.~ She dragged him off, following her brother's footing with ease.

Camer stood at the entrance of a small cave, Mattias running back towards him. 'Behind you, Caya!' he shouted, pointing.

Caya looked back and saw a great wave of bright blue light sweeping up the hillside. It completely filled her gaze, nothing visible beyond it, and there was no end to it.

She turned back, with heightened resolve. By then, Mattias had reached them and helped her help Qyan. Together, they speedily made their way to the cave, barely making it inside when the wave struck the entrance.

Qyan sank down in a heap, his eyes closed. Caya lay her cloak over him gently and glared at Mattias 'What in Kaisha's name was that?' she asked angrily.

Note to readers:

Kaisha was one of the six Great Dragons and was responsible for the bringing of Life. She existed at the time of the creation of the realms alongside the other five Great Dragons.

Kaisha's name is invoked in a similar way to the way the fourth-realmers use 'God' or 'heaven'. Only when the situation pertains to a life-threatening situation will Kaisha's, or Rectys's name be invoked. Rectys was responsible for the bringing of Death and his name is only mentioned under the worst circumstances. In many cultures, his name is forgotten.

The other four Great Dragons were Trya, of Water, Drôn, of Fire, Nårio, of Air, and, Berak of Earth. More will be learned of them as the story continues, as they play a vital part in the lives of the Children of Destiny.

To resume:

'That,' Mattias said slowly, 'was a shift change. A natural, and deadly phenomenon of the realm that only has any effect upon Jumpers not born to this realm. All Jumpers are eradicated on contact with that friendly-looking blue light. There are warnings all around the towns for non-natives to get into caves or buildings if in the realm during a shift change. It is believed that the light is caused by a shift in the realm's magickal field and balance has to be restored. It marks the changes from the 'day-shift' to 'night-shift' for all the workers as well, although the times between each change vary greatly.'

Caya continued to quiz Mattias, annoyed at his blatant complacency with regard to their situation.

Camer shook his head at the pair and crouched next to Qyan. 'Hey, you ok?' he asked, concerned at the boy's ashen face.

Darkness

Qyan shook his head to clear the sweeping dizziness that had overtaken him. *~I will be. I just need to rest. I just... ~* The connection broke off as Qyan's energy drained further, the Water Elementalist drifting into a deep sleep once more.

Mattias shrugged. 'Well, that's that. You've survived your first shift change. Be glad that you did, as it is rare among many Jumpers who travel unguided.'

Caya shook her head and looked at Camer, still annoyed at her brother. 'So what should we do now? Is it safe?'

Camer nodded 'It is safe to venture outside if you want to. But surely we should wait for your friend to recover?'

'How about we finish our business here in Dra'noxia and then go and find Scortia. We have two months. Possibly longer.'

Caya shook her head. 'Let's rest for now and decide what to do in the morning.'

'What morning?' Mattias asked. 'The suns never set. They just rotate randomly around the sky. There is no fixed length to the day. We've been trying to figure it out for ages.'

'Fine,' Caya muttered. 'Morning for Catré.'

'Good idea.' Camer smiled faintly before settling down, leaving Mattias to take the first watch.

Mattias sighed, watching his friend drift into the unfathomable realms of sleep. The constant sunlight was annoying him and he longed for the comfort of sunset and the moonlight. He stared out at the silent, sunlit expanse that led down to Dra'noxia. The town was bustling with the latest business. The place never paused, never had a moment of peace. But the sounds from the city never reached further than the beginning of the slopes.

The boy yawned, glancing at his sleeping companions, wondering how he got lumped with first watch. The silence was lonely and intense, uncannily noticeable. But due to this, he noticed the sudden break in the quiet. Something was moving nearby the cave, unnatural for the area. They were the only people in the vicinity, all other places of shelter being at least ten minutes walk away. Silently, he drew his sword, rising to his feet.

He frowned, creeping up to the entrance, peering out cautiously. But still, he could see nothing, although the sound continued.

He stepped out slowly, his eyes roaming the landscape, his whole body tense, alert to sudden movements. He was only a few feet from the cave's

Darkness

entrance. Scanning the valley completely, he frowned, seeing nothing out of the ordinary. The grassy hills were devoid of any movement. Sighing, he sheathed his sword again and moved back to the cave, wondering if the tiredness was just making him hear things.

It must have been a small animal, he thought to himself, taking great pleasure in the sensation of stepping from the intense heat back into the cool shade the cave provided.

He kept watch for a further three marks, timing it carefully on his watch. The day barely changed while the others slept.

When his time was up, he turned and woke Camer quietly to take his place the moment his watch clicked past the third mark of his watch. He was tired and settled down to sleep almost instantly.

Camer woke reasonably quickly and took his place, slipping Mattias's watch from the sleeping boy's wrist to keep time himself. He sat at the cave entrance, his hand resting on the hilt of his sword the whole time. He could feel someone else watching them, but saw nothing himself. During the full three marks, nothing of interest occurred, although his unease grew with every passing moment.

After a while longer, he rose from his position, walking over to wake Caya so she could take the third watch.

Caya started, her hand jumping to her sword. Seeing Camer, however, calmed her again. She rubbed the sleep from her eyes and took up her position. As Camer settled down to rest, she half-drew her sword, keeping it ready as she peered out into the day.

~*What is it?*~ Camer asked, his hand finding his sword as he heard her sword.

~*There is something out there. Wake Mattias. We will let Qyan rest unless we need to wake him,*~ she replied, unmoving.

~*I don't hear anything,*~ Camer noted. ~*But I sensed something, all through my watch. It's unnerving, but I saw nothing.*~ He moved towards Mattias, quietly.

~*Neither do I, but eyes can deceive. Use your element. Something has disturbed the moisture in the air far beyond the power of the wind.*~

Camer shook his friend awake, quickly putting a hand to his mouth to silence him. ~*Quiet. We have a problem,*~ he explained, nodding towards the valley outside.

Caya tightened her grip on her sword. ~*It's moving slowly and silently and clearly does not want to be seen, so it is definitely not just a passer-by,*~ she frowned. ~*It knows we are here, whatever it is. I doubt it has good intentions either.*~ She stood slowly, moving to a more sheltered spot at the mouth of the cave, her eyes never leaving the area outside. *~Mattias. Can you stand right here. Keep your guard up. I am going to open a Gate.~*

Mattias took her place as she moved further into the cave. *~What about the noise?~* he asked.

~Leave that to me.~

Camer was quick to interrupt her work. *~Gates can be traced. They can just follow us.~*

Caya frowned before resuming her work. *~Leave that to me. How many can they trace at once?~*

~Up to three I think. Maybe more.~

Caya nodded, drawing five symbols in the air, followed by the silencing symbol. Opening the Gate, she was glad to have drawn it correctly, no noise audible. She repeated the process, opening Gate after Gate within each other.

~Will that work?~ Camer asked, watching her.

~It had better, but in all honesty, I don't know,~ Caya replied as she opened the sixth Gate. She focussed on the seventh, her choice of destination being: *Somewhere they won't follow. Somewhere we can hide.* She pulled it open, wondering if a location would be revealed with such a vague instruction. *~Go. Get out while I can hold it.~*

Camer dragged Qyan through as carefully as he

could without compromising speed. The pair disappeared into the white light.

Mattias backed up towards the Gates. ~*We have company,*~ he told her.

Caya looked back out at Cyphia and gasped as a black form blocked the light. It was large, almost filling the entrance to the cave, and it had two pairs of fly-like wings. The brightness of the sunlight behind it made it impossible for her to make out any other features and she stumbled back through her Gates as it approached. Once through, she shut them all at once. The cave becoming a white light before fading out to a homely room.

She looked around and saw the others staring at her from the corner of the room, and she was glad to see them all safe. Qyan was awake and on his feet, although he still looked exhausted.

It did not take her very long to realise something. *They aren't looking at me. They are looking at something behind me.* And with that sudden thought, she span around and saw a woman standing there.

'Is this everyone?' the stranger asked. At their lack of movement, she smiled. 'Good. I'm Drásda. Drásda Mîchka. Now who's hungry? I was about to cook some dinner.'

Wings.
Beating wings.
We can soar.

Through the Void.
Among the emptiness.

Chapter 6

Drazdéré

Maytra wondered aimlessly about the Letran camp, wondering of what use she was. Lee had settled in and had many good friends amongst the soldiers, working with many of those who held similar values to their two prior leaders: Scarien, and then briefly, Mattias.

Lyana had asked the pair to help around with any odd-jobs they could find, but Maytra was struggling with the way of life. She could not settle down as easily as her son, nor could she be of any use when she tried to help out. In fact, she often gave others even more work than they had to begin with.

Lee ran past and paused to greet his mother. 'Hey. I'm just going to help Jasor. It's nearly lunchtime and he's struggling.'

Maytra hugged her son briefly. 'Okay. Take care in that kitchen. You know how wild it can get,' she advised before watching him dart off. Over the past few days they had been helping with work around the section that Mattias had led previously, many other groups seeming more scornful and hard to approach. The people there were welcoming enough, but for Maytra, she felt like she did not belong among them, knowing that her home lay elsewhere, lost forever.

'Maytra!'

She turned around at the call in time to see Qyesar running over to her.

'How are you today?' he asked.

She nodded slightly. 'I'm fine. Could be worse,' she replied.

'They'll be fine,' he said assuredly, knowing what was bothering her. 'You shouldn't worry so much. Anyway, I've been asked to tell you that Lyana would like to see you after lunch today.'

'What about Lee?'

'I'll keep an eye on him for you. I could use an extra pair of hands and he is ever so keen.'

She thanked him and they walked to lunch together. Just as they arrived, the daily debate started up, even while people were still collecting their food.

Curious, Maytra listened, choosing not to take part

herself.

Qyesar plated her up some food, as well as getting his own, and nodded to a seat. 'You'll hear better there. Close but not too close to lose your plate.' He smiled warmly.

'We're not necessarily the smartest race. All races are smart in their own ways. Take the fourth-realmers for example. Look at everything they created. We can use their technology, but only because they found the way to create it,' Francin argued.

Braedor, one of the opposition, laughed. 'But they gave up magick. Where was the sense in that? If they were smart, they would have remained among their own. Magick is everything for us.'

'Fair point, but you cannot deny what they have given us. Blame not the descendants. Maybe magick became too much for their ancestors. They needed a way out.

'Besides, there are also the Clorans. They could create magick. It is thanks to them we have control over the Elements,' countered Francin.

'But does that really make them smart? If they were smart, then where are they now? Those who escaped, died. I would not call that very smart. They couldn't cure a simple disease. Their stupidity was in keeping themselves cut off from other realms.'

'That disease was resistant to all magick. Maybe we could have learnt from the medicines of the fourth-realm. And do not blame the Clorans. Their realm should never have been the battlefield of others.'

'They still died, did they not?'

Maytra stood up, deciding to take a stand for once. She had listened to their debates every day so far. 'You think all the Clorans died? Maybe they are that much smarter than the Elementalists to stay hidden. Everywhere you go, you hear tales of the Elementalists. Someone always knows where you are. I call that stupidity.'

Braedor turned to her. 'And what would a simple Catréan know about this? You people rarely know much from beyond your own realm.'

Maytra shook her head. 'Maybe I don't know, maybe I do. After all, what Catréan can do this?'

She picked up a plate and began to work it into a malleable material, changing its very essence. She shaped it swiftly, a perfect scale model of the Citadel of Tresh sitting in the palm of her hand. Even the swirling Ora had been mimicked, though the magick was not wild inside it. The patterns were still intoxicating, but she quickly dulled them so none could be lost to the statue. 'After all, I'm just a

Darkness

Catréan. I know nothing.'

She turned away from the astonished faces, glad to notice that Braedor was bemused, his entire argument blown apart. She told Qyesar that she was going to see Lyana and left with a smile.

As she walked, she played with the statue until it was just a small clay ball, similar in size to the one already in her pocket. She smiled inwardly, having enjoyed putting some speculations right. It had been her duty, after all.

Lyana had turned the room next to Scarien's office into a very similar office, trying to make it as comfortable as possible for all. When Maytra entered, she looked up from the paperwork she was busy with and smiled. Standing, she walked over and embraced the woman.

'I'm glad you could come.' She waved a hand around the office. 'What do you think?' she asked.

'I like it. Similar, but not so much that it feels wrong,' she replied, looking around and noticing the small bowls of water around the place. 'It is rather a relaxing room.' She looked at Lyana, wondering what she had actually been called for.

'That's what just about everyone has said so far. I didn't think it would be right to have an exact replica. Even I would have been uncomfortable in a room that looked the same.' She indicated a chair. 'Please, have a seat.'

Maytra sat herself down, Lyana walking back to her desk. After sorting some paperwork into a drawer, she turned back to the Cloran.

'We know where the boys and Caya are. We feel it would be to your benefit if you joined them for a while. They are with someone it is crucial for you to meet, especially at this moment in time. Your part is yet to be played. I highly doubt that coincidence placed Scortia in your care. Had she not, you may never have come this far.'

'What about Scortia? Do you know where she is?' Maytra asked, struggling to keep her voice steady.

'We do not know. We know that she is no longer with the Zyrons, and we also know that she is not with the other three. We believe, however, that she is with the rest of her missing team-mates and we are searching for them as we speak now.'

Maytra nodded. 'So who is this person I should meet?'

'Her name is Drásda Mîchka. She got in touch with us a few years ago, letting us know that her services were available if ever required. We kept her location secret for her and she has assisted us where she can. She contacted us only a few hours ago to let us know that the three are with her now.'

Maytra frowned at the name. 'Do I know her?'

'You should. You escaped Cloric with her. She is also a Cloran. Your cousin, to be precise.'

'Cousin?'

'According to what she has told us. She is anxious to meet you once more.'

'What about my son?'

'He can accompany you if you wish, or he can stay here under our care. I have noticed that he has many friends among the soldiers.

'I have a feeling that you would rather he did not accompany you. He is very special, your son, and he knows his own way. Drazdéré is no place for him, and the burden Drásda bears may weigh him down.'

Maytra looked uncertain, weighing her options carefully. The Letran made sense, but she dreaded leaving her son behind. There were a few she would trust with him, however.

'I'll go,' she said slowly, 'but Lee stays with Jasor, Qyesar, Daesir, Francin or yourself at all times. At least then I know he is with someone I can trust to keep him safe.'

Lyana nodded. 'As long as it is in my power, he will

be with one of us.'

Maytra smiled anxiously. 'Thank you.' She began to draw the symbols for a Gate, before realising that she did not know the destination.

'Allow me,' smiled Lyana, intervening. Swiftly, she opened the Gate and watched as Maytra stepped through before closing it behind her.

After a moment, she smiled, sending a messenger to gather up the four soldiers as well as Lee. They all had to be told of the arrangements. It would be wrong not to follow through with her promise.

* * * * * * * * * * * *

The children sat around the table, the tumblers before them filled with a cool, dark liquid. The woman who had greeted them was bustling around the room, making sure they were comfortable.

After several minutes of the four just looking at each other, Qyan decided to voice the question they were all asking. 'What realm is this?'

The woman did not answer for a while, preparing her own drink. When she did turn, she sat herself down next to Mattias and smiled. 'I am sorry. I was under the impression that you already knew.' She drank a little of her drink before continuing. 'This is the twelfth realm, Drazdéré.'

The four froze, Camer choking on his drink.

Qyan rubbed his head slightly, feeling more than worse-for-wear, but looked stoically across the table at Drásda. 'But surely nobody lives on Drazdéré. No one sane, I mean. This excludes the Dracona.'

'Normally, you would be right. But it is an ideal place to hide from the realms. The Dracona are not at all bad so long as you keep out of their way. A couple bring me food each day, and I make them things in return. It was the Dracona who showed me this cave to stay in. It only took a little work to make it more comfortable.

From outside came the sound of rustling wings. Drásda excused herself from the table with a smile and went to the door, pulling it quickly open. 'Amerita!' she exclaimed happily. 'Please, come in. We have guests today.'

The one called Amerita stepped inside slowly. She was very pale with hair so dark it was almost black. From her back sprouted two leathery wings which slowly shrank away from view. She smiled warmly at the children.

'We have been expecting you for some months now. What delayed you so?' she asked gently.

Studying them carefully, she frowned and walked over to Qyan, her tone suddenly colder as she spoke. 'You are not one of them. Where is the fourth? Who are you?'

Qyan looked her in the eyes. 'My name is Qyan Aguana. I am here to help find Scortia and the rest of our team.'

The Dracona frowned, clearly taken aback by the boy's obvious lack of fear. Deciding to test him, she fully Morphed in an instant, her wings appearing and arching threateningly, her eyes becoming large and serpentine, and her pale skin turning into blue and white scales, hands and feet now claws. She sent a spurt of fire towards him, the stream passing him by, but only by an inch.

Qyan did not flinch, still steadily meeting her gaze. Truth be told, he was still too exhausted to care. The others, however, backed against the wall, fear showing clear in their faces.

Slightly perturbed, she sent a spurt directly at him, but he just lifted a hand, catching it in a ball of water, the entire creation spinning before him. He reversed the spin, sending it back to her, knowing that it would do no damage.

Returning to her usual form, Amerita could not help but smile warmly. 'You have a Dragon's heart,' she said with clear satisfaction in her voice. 'If you would follow me. We have a way that you may find your friends. After all, the fourth cannot remain missing. You are needed.'

The group stood together, their drinks now empty. Amerita made her way back to the door and went to open it. However, she stopped the way; distracted by something they could all hear.

A Gate was opening. There was no mistaking that sound. Amerita Morphed almost instantly, positioning herself in front of the group, ready to attack. As a woman stepped through, she tensed.

Drásda ran forward. 'No. Do not attack!' she cried, grabbing the Dracona by her shoulders. 'It is my cousin.'

Caya frowned in recognition, unsure of what Drásda meant. She looked curiously at Drásda, confused. 'Cousin?'

Drásda stepped forward, hugging the woman tight. 'Maytra. You came. I had almost lost hope of seeing you again until the Letrans told me you were there. I have missed you more than you could imagine.'

Maytra stood back from her cousin, pulling free of the embrace and frowning. 'I don't remember anything.'

'After everything you went through, no one can blame you for that.'

'What happened?'

'You will learn, my cousin. But now is not the time. It is good that you are here. I need you to help me.'

Before Maytra could ask any questions, Amerita de-Morphed, looking slightly put out. She walked back to the door, pulling it open. 'Let us go and find the fourth child, and the others.' With that, she stepped outside into the gleaming moonlight.

As Caya followed, she could not help but admire the realm. It seemed so peaceful. Everywhere she looked, there was just unspoilt landscape, illuminated by the moonlight and seeming to glow silver as a result.

Towards the north, the sun was beginning to rise as they walked. Amerita scowled as she saw this and pulled them quickly inside a cave. It seemed to just open up behind them.

They could see how the plants had adapted to the intense sunlight, some curling up and vanishing into the ground as soon as the sunrays touched them, others being a strange reddish-gold colour, reflecting a lot of the light away. This golden coating also seemed to keep them cool, clearly not conducting the heat.

Even in the shade, the group could feel the intense heat of the rapidly rising sun.

'Animals only ever venture out at night. It only takes

minutes for the sun to kill you. Some do dart from cave to cave, but only when the route is well known. Lose a cave and there is nothing that can save you.' She scowled, watching a young Dracona dart across the landscape. 'It is always the young. Daring and foolish as they are.'

They watched as he dove into a cave, his scales seeming to smoke. He waited there, recovering but clearly planning his next move.

Shaking her head, Amerita turned and led them back through the cave. 'We will have to take the long way around. Every cave links to the tunnels. The tunnel network is safer than the sun.'

The sides of the path were lined with different coloured stalagmites and stalactites. The colours shone bright and, in their luminescence, they lit the way ahead with a gentle soft light.

The caves themselves were pleasantly dry and a small purple stream ran uphill on their left, and a pinker one ran downhill on their right. Both were also glowing brightly, the waters silent.

Every now and then, a strange small animal would cross their path, disappearing quickly into the small crevices. Some had shining colours of their own, while others were almost invisible, adapted in their own ways to the lives they led.

As the group walked on, the reds, blues and purples became much more prominent against the other colours, making the whole room seem to glow violet. Shortly after, a vast cavern appeared, lined with various tunnels, each opening into the cavern with its own dominant shade. The cavern floor was far below them; the only way down for those walking being a path that wound around the walls. The path itself was bright yellow, showing up clearly against the darker walls. Every other entrance to the cavern was bustling with Dracona walking and flying in and out.

Note to readers:

I apologise sincerely for the level of descriptiveness here, but as you become to understand the nature of the Dracona as this tale continues, you will come to understand why every detail is important. Colour creates their world. To see it wrong is to firstly, do them an injustice, and secondly may cause confusion later.

The colours are all natural and they were the main reason the Dracona evolved the way they have. So far, the mysteries of the cavern's origins have been unexplained.

To resume:

Halfway down to the bottom, the group were

stopped by one of the many guards. Amerita quickly said something to him in her own tongue and he nodded, flying over to the other side. They entered one of the tunnels, following its winding route to a much greener cavern. Here, they made their way to the bottom and took a seat.

'We have to wait to be called. Many Lose things in the tunnel network. Here is where they are Found.' Her voice seemed to automatically capitalise the words 'lose' and 'found', as though they meant much more than reality suggested.

The children nodded and engaged in private conversation, finding out more about each other. Having not had a chance before to properly talk in Cyphia, it was the perfect opportunity. Many things were discussed, including their past and what they knew of the prophecy and their place among the Elementalists. They all had a long story to tell and asked many questions of each other. Caya asked Mattias and Camer a lot about Scarien Éscaronôvic, curious to learn more about her father. In return, she and Qyan were quizzed on their time with the Zyrons and the tournaments.

The three adults shared a glance, smiling slightly and keeping themselves out of the conversation. After a while, however, Maytra could not help but ask her cousin questions about the Clorans, trying to retrieve her memories. She felt as if she was missing out on a chapter of her life, and that the false memories she had subconsciously created to fill the gaps made her entire life and existence a lie.

Drásda was hesitant at first to answer, not wishing to dwell on such topics, but she recognised the woman's need to know and eventually caved in, discussing their lives and events they had shared.

Maytra smiled, listening for the most part, but asking more and more questions, trying to force her old memories to surface, but to no avail. That part of her life was long since buried and she sensed that the pain may prove too much for her.

'Amerita!' the guard called. 'Cast Three is ready for you.'

The Dracona woman stood and smiled. 'Time for us to move from here,' she said, leading the way down more tunnels.

The children stood quickly, agreeing to continue their conversation later, eager to find the others. They followed her carefully, not liking these tunnels as they had the previous; they were cold, dark and damp, lit only by dim torches. They were far from welcoming to them.

Darkness

They soon entered a large room with a huge gem protruding from the centre of the floor. It did not seem to have been cut into its shape, but it was flawless and perfectly shaped. Equally spaced around this wonder, were five fully-Morphed Dracona, identical to one another save for eye colour. Their vast golden wings just touched the ones next to them at the tips.

As one, the five turned to greet the group. The movement was in perfect time and was eerie. The one nearest the group retracted his wings, stepping forward out of formation.

'Who is the Seeker?' he asked, his voice glittering in the air in a way only the highest Dracona could achieve.

Caya and Qyan were nudged forward by Amerita. She murmured something softly to them and they spoke together.

'We are. We Seek those who we have lost. The connection we share is greater than that of just a friend.'

'Place your hands on the Finder. Bring those you Seek to the forefront of your mind and focus solely on them.'

Amerita nodded towards the gem and the pair stepped up to it, placing their hands on the smooth surface. Behind them, the Dracona moved back to his place and the five regained their formation around the wing, silent.

From each of the golden Dracona, two thin golden lines spread over the Finder, forming a glowing pentagram.

The gem itself began to pulse with a soft blue light, an image forming in the air above it. There was Qwenox, looking extremely distressed.

Caya tried to step back from the gem, but her hands seemed to be glued to it by a strange force. She watched as Haero threw fireball after fireball at the wall of what could only be described as a cell. His attempts achieved nothing, but served to tire him. Xanor pulled the boy back and down to join the rest of the group.

A shadow filled the image, blocking their view before the whole spectacle faded away.

The golden Dracona did not move, but Qyan and Caya fell back as if the gem had shoved their hands away.

As the pair rejoined the others, the Dracona who had spoken before turned back to them and spoke in his sparkling voice. 'Go now and forget your friends. There is nothing more you can do.'

Another turned, continuing in exactly the same voice. 'Along the road to their freedom lies almost certain death.'

A third took up the speech. 'Their captors are ruthless and would sooner kill their prisoners at any hint of rescue, than risk escape.'

The fourth added slowly, as if he was reluctant to do so, but compelled to anyway. 'The first realm, Haveen, is where you will find them. In the Valley of the Light. But only when darkness fills the land.'

The fifth finished. 'The cave that never opens holds a secret you must uncover. Only then can there be hope for your task.'

Note to readers:

As I am sure you are querying the Draconas' statement, I feel it is my duty to explain a minor fact here.

The Dracona, or Searchers as some call them, are incapable of lying. They can only do their duty to Find what is Lost. As they deem it part of their duty, they will often dissuade the Seeker from continuing along their road. They can often see the immediate consequence of going to Find the person or item and therefore, will share their knowledge cryptically.

In this case, however, the fifth Dracona, who rarely speaks, has also Found something of consequence. He cannot know if what he Finds is directly related, but treats it as though it is. Indeed, in this case, he may be looking further ahead.

On another note, the gemstone, the Finder, is of a substance harder than diamond and purer than the cleanest water. It is found naturally this way and cannot be cut into its shape. The Dracona seem to have found a way to manipulate the gem, but it is unclear how.

The Finder is considered, to the Dracona, to be a stone of protection and fortuity. The shards that are left, after shaping the Finder to work at its best, are given to newborn Dracona as a pendant on a chain. They wear these chains for the rest of their lives and even after Death. Each is unique and responds only to their true owners. Such uncut shards would be worth millions in Earth should they ever be exported out of Drazdéré to other realms.

To resume:

Amerita bowed slightly before leading the others out and back through the tunnels. Mattias frowned, looking pensive.

'What did they mean? Why the warnings?' he asked after an uneasy silence.

'They will always provide their own advice, based on fact. They cannot stop you from doing anything, and always give you the information you seek, but they often provide extra information to prepare you,' Amerita replied hastily. 'You should heed their warning, but I sense you will not.'

'No!' Caya quickly interjected. 'We have to do anything we can.'

'Very well. I will lead you to the Gate room. We can get provisions for you along the way.'

'Are you coming with us?' the girl then asked.

'I don't know,' she replied, pausing. She turned, looking at the group, her wings appearing. 'I doubt I can acquire permission, but you will need a guide, and I do know the realm in question.'

'Do try,' Mattias said, 'We will need someone with us, and we would be sad to see you leave so soon.' He could sense the others nodding in agreement, though his eyes were on the Dracona.

Drásda added, 'A guide would be invaluable. And you are a dear friend to me. You always wanted an adventure. Take the chance.'

Amerita nodded. 'I will try, but I make no promises.' and she leapt up, her wings stretching out as she flew off, leaving the group to explore at their own leisure.

Caya and Qyan followed the path back to the first tunnel to examine the streams. Camer and Mattias followed closely, taking in their surroundings and debating the level of naturalness. Mattias was of the opinion that it had been sculpted, but Camer insisted otherwise.

Drásda watched them with a slight frown and she turned to Maytra. 'Well, I guess it is just you and me,' she smiled, sitting down on the ground.

* * * * * * * * * * * * *

Qyan frowned, flummoxed by the streams. ~*It is water, but at the same time, it is not. It is more conscious, almost alive.*~

~*Do you mean that it is a mixture with water and other substances besides?*~ Camer asked, confused.

Caya shook her head, sensing the same as Qyan. ~*All of it is water, yet all of it is not.*~

This only served to confuse the two spectators even more and so Qyan raised the liquid as he normally would Water.

~*It is wrong. It is water. It acts like water, save for moving uphill, and in feels like water. It even responds like water. However, while being so close to water, it is almost the opposite,*~ he frowned.

Caya continued, ~*We can only work with water. If it is not water, we cannot manipulate it on the same level. In that respect, this substance is water. However, we can feel the make-up of water, we can feel its essence, and this is different. Therefore, it is not water.*~

The two Elementalists turned to face each other. ~*It is like the negative of Water,*~ they said together.

Darkness

~We see...~ Camer and Mattias replied, although truthfully, they were more confused than before.

* * * * * * * * * * * *

Amerita joined back up with the group, smiling warmly. The children had since left the strange liquid and rejoined the Clorans.

'I can accompany you,' Amerita said happily. 'The Shiners believed it is a suicide mission, but our queen said otherwise and sent me with you to guide and protect.' She had brought several large packs, one for each person and each containing food, water, clothing and some small weapons.

'How did you carry all this?' Camer asked, slinging the pack onto his back, the weight bearing him down at first.

'The Dracona are born of the Air. We can manipulate it to suit our basic needs, just not to the extent of the Elementalists themselves.'

The children helped each other arrange their current possessions into the new packs. They seemed large at first, but after a moment of wearing them, they barely noticed their presence. Amerita nodded in satisfaction and smiled when they thanked her.

The Dracona turned, leading the group out to the Gate room, a large blue-ish chamber. There was a circle of seats around the edge for all those waiting for an arrival.

Caya began drawing the symbols to open a Gate and wove in the silencing spell. Pulling it open, she felt the strain that Jared had warned her of. She had not felt it before; presumably the adrenaline had given her that extra rush.

She held the Gate open for the others to step through. The Dracona paused, taking one backwards glance at her home before joining them all on Haveen, the Gate swinging shut and vanishing behind her.

My name.
Once it would invoke fear.
For others it invoked awe.

Now.
Now it is forgotten.
That will change.
This name will live on.

Chapter 7

Inheritance

The members of Qwenox were thrown mercilessly into a dark, damp cell. From what little they had seen of their captors, they could not make any valid assumptions on race, but they knew they had never seen such beings before. They also knew that they had been taken through many Gates and had no indication as to what realm they were in.

Iano and Barek searched the cell together. They examined every wall and the floor and ceiling to find some weak spot in the rock. The bars, themselves were impenetrable, but there were several areas in the wall. However, the structure was so strong and thick that it would take a lot of time and effort to make their way out. Also, the wall seemed to dampen their range of sensing, so they had no idea what lay beyond their prison, or how thick the wall actually was.

~We'll be here a while. We might as well take our time over this one. Otherwise we will be too exhausted to escape,~ Barek murmured, keeping even his mental voice quiet.

Scortia nodded. ~Meanwhile, we should act the part of children: frustrated and terrified. Otherwise, they will suspect us.~

The group nodded and settled into their roles quickly, ready for any guards. After all, they could not sense when they were approaching. To be perfectly honest, there was very little acting required.

The first guard entered the room after several hours, settling in a seat, watching them through the bars, ready for any escape attempts. His gaze was scrutinising.

Though the team was surprised at his appearance, none of them showed it. He was very tall and his skin was black with course black hairs all over. His arms had three joints rather than one, and instead of hands, he had pincer-like claws. Similarly, his legs had too many joints and were unnaturally spindly with feet similar to his hands, but much smaller. His face seemed normal save for the strange skin and his huge bulbous eyes.

As he sat, they caught a glimpse of two-pairs of transparent wings, great black veins spreading throughout them. They were papery-thin, but so large that it was strange that they had not noticed them earlier.

Darkness

~Havern,~ Xanor warned, ~I've only heard a little about them, but our situation is looking a lot worse. This is not a race to mess with.~

Haero stood, moving towards the bars, his temper rising as his stomach rumbled. His hunger outweighed Xanor's words, his young arrogance shining through. 'Hey! We're starving in here. Get us something to eat,' he shouted at the guard.

'You speak Veena?' the guard asked in a gruff voice, not reacting otherwise to the boy. He was clearly surprised at being able to understand them.

'No. I speak Xerd,' Haero replied, 'Now we want food.'

'What?' Scortia asked, looking confused, 'But I speak Costra. How can we all understand each other?'

Nesqo could not help but smile, despite their situation. He enjoyed knowing more than his companions. 'As far as I am aware, even those of us speaking Xerd are speaking different dialects. And yet, we have always understood each other.'

Note to readers:

It is true that every person in this room is speaking in their own tongue. It is also true that they have always been able to understand each other despite this. This is due to the principle of realm-jumping. All Jumpers gain an ability to understand the languages being spoken around them, and enables those around to understand what they are saying. It is really a side-effect, but it is a useful one, allowing the Jumpers to make the transition from one realm to another without any barriers.

The reason the Elementalists all understand each other, despite never realm-jumping before is because they are in a realm that is not their own. This has the same effect as Jumping itself.

To resume:

This only confused Scortia further and she wondered how it could be possible. The guard was also becoming very confused, and consequently, he flew into a furious rage. Launching himself at the bars, he shook them manically. Out of his mouth came a string of nonsensical syllables, spraying them with his extremely acidic saliva.

The group moved as far back as possible, their skin itching and, in the worst-hit spots, burning. Due to the shock of the sudden sensation, they initially screamed, desperately trying to wipe it off.

Suddenly, the guard was calm, an evil glint in his eyes. He stared at Nesqo, a smile appearing and broadening rapidly as a vein pulsed in his eye.

Nesqo's head snapped around sickeningly, forcing him to stare straight back at the Havern. The boy released a strangled cry as the Havern's power waxed, fed by the fear filling the room. The others could do little but watch as their team-mate struggled to fight free.

Staring at her friend's face, Scortia could not bear it. She quickly connected her mind to his, trying to block out the pain. She could feel what he was suffering and it distracted her from her task. *How has he kept fighting this long already?* she wondered. She eventually managed to block out the pain and focussed on forcing back the intruder.

Nesqo felt her attempts and as his free-will began to return, he joined her efforts. Together, they were strong enough to force the Havern out and to escape his iron grip.

Once released, every member of the team threw up solid barriers in their minds, backing away further from the bars. Not one dared to speak, knowing a single word could potentially provoke the clearly unstable warden.

The Havern just smiled at them cruelly and settled back into the chair as though nothing had happened. The faint glow from his eyes faded as he dozed. After barely a moment, it flared back into existence as he took a final look at the group, before fading back to nothing. He twitched slightly as he slipped into a deep, black sleep.

Haero stood and faced the wall, his frustration

growing. He conjured fireballs, throwing them repeatedly at the surface. Although his attacks were powerful, they did little more than char the surface. This did not dissuade the boy and his attacks got more fierce, each strike exploding on the wall.

The guard sat up and growled, awakened by the noise. Xanor hurriedly grabbed Haero, pulling him down to sit with the rest of the group. They all watched fearfully as the guard returned to his sleep.

Xanor kept a firm grip on the boy. *He's too young for this. We need to look out for him,* he thought to himself, sighing.

Scortia watched sympathetically, reflecting on the past few months. It seemed like only yesterday she was arguing with her mother and walking out the door. Only yesterday when she was drawn up the mountain in a beautiful pink storm.

Only she was never my mother, Scortia thought to herself. *But that storm was beautiful. Almost magickal. What would have happened if I had never gone up that mountain? I wouldn't be here. I would be safe and warm at Caya's house. If only I had stuck to my original plan. If only I hadn't been so impulsive. If only ... 'If only's will get me nowhere...*

She looked up, breaking away from the train of thought, something odd catching her eye. A shadow flitted across the room, barely noticeable. Blinking, she turned her head, deciding she was seeing things, but it passed by again. Staring more intently, she saw nothing. There was only wall.

A scant moment later, a boy appeared, followed by a man. They seemed to melt out of the shadows. The man smiled gently at the group in the cell while the boy checked the guard.

'He's asleep already,' the boy whispered. 'I have given him a small dose to keep him that way until we are clear.'

The man nodded and relaxed slightly. 'Good Vlökir.' He turned to the team, melting into the cell in his shadowy way. 'You have friends waiting for you. My name is Xophîn. We must hurry before the Havern find you gone. Follow my son, and do not let go of each other.'

Vlökir slipped into the cell also and ripped a hole into the shadows. Grabbing Nesqo's hand, he stepped through, dragging the boy with him. Nesqo quickly grabbed onto Haero and the team formed a chain with Xophîn at the end.

As Barek slipped through, Iano and Scortia gulped, more guards spilling into the cell. Their wings seemed to be pulsing. And then they were gone, replaced by the gloom of shadow.

It was a strange sensation, passing through the darkness. It was like being pulled through water, only the substance was thicker and dry, almost ghost-like in nature. They could see nothing, only barely able to feel each other's touch. There was only shadow.

* * * * * * * * * * * *

Amerita led the group towards the Valley of the Light. It was aptly named. It was by far the brightest place any of them had set their eyes on. The sun was reflected by mirror-like sheets of cascading water, the spray creating dazzling colourful patterns in the air. It was a wide bowl with a narrow crevice leading out for the water to leave by.

Camer frowned, the ground being of a substance he could not identify. It, too, was like a mirror, smooth and flawless.

Despite the brightness of the place, they all could not help but shudder and step back. It stank of evil, the light masking something utterly dark and corrupt.

Drásda lay a hand on Maytra's shoulder. 'It is our time to depart. We cannot continue down this road. We can return to the Letrans and collect your son. But there is much to do before the time is right and time is running out.'

Maytra hesitated, so close to seeing Scortia once more, but there was truth in her cousin's words. The two Clorans made their farewells before turning and walking back across the landscape.

Amerita watched the pair until they were long out of sight. Nodding, she turned back, leading the children down into the dazzling valley.

'There is the entrance to their hive, but it never opens,' Amerita whispered, pointing to a hollow in the ground. 'I do not know if it is the cave the Seekers were speaking of, but we cannot go any closer to it, else they will detect our presence.'

Qyan sat down, puzzling it over. 'This place is wrong,' he commented, watching the valley before him.

Mattias frowned, having an idea. He spoke silently with Camer, the conversation brief, before turning to the others.

'Xophîn,' he said softly.

Caya looked confused. 'What?' she asked, wondering what this had to do with rescuing the others.

'Xophîn,' he repeated, louder than before. It was as if he were calling someone.

'At your service, young Mattias.'

Caya jumped, jolting around. Amerita instantly Morphed, reacting to the presence of another. Sure enough, standing merely a few steps away, was a man. It was a man who had apparently materialised from nothing.

Mattias ignored her astonishment, talking quickly but quietly, ever aware of their precarious position. 'Xophîn, we need to ask a favour of you. Do you think you can manage?'

Xophîn nodded, listening carefully to the situation. This was something no other race could do, and he smiled at the task he was given, such was his enjoyment at taking on a challenge. Calling his son to the area, he vanished back into shadow.

* * * * * * * * * * * *

Vlökir led the group out into a bright valley where five others were waiting anxiously. The sensation of leaving shadow made Scortia feel like she had been pushed through a very narrow opening that could not quite fit her size. It was not painful, though, just uncomfortable.

Caya was quick to embrace her team-mates, Qyan greeting each warmly, at least, warmly for him. They took several moments to catch up and get back into their team spirit.

Xanor frowned. ~*You look dreadful, Qyan,*~ he said, commenting on the tired and drawn expression. ~*You should have stayed in bed longer.*~

~*No, thank you. I could not stay there a moment longer. It is searching for you that takes its toll. I still have a lot of connections to make, but you all decided to vanish.*~

Barek and Iano both spoke together, voicing the thought of most of the group. Nodding towards Mattias, Camer and Amerita, they asked, ~*Who are they?*~

Caya clapped a hand to her forehead. 'Sorry, I almost forgot,' she said, speaking aloud for Amerita's sake. Turning towards the others, she introduced them to the team. 'This is Mattias, our brother. Camer, his friend. And Amerita, a Dracona who has been helping us find you lot.'

The three nodded as their names were spoken, indicating who they were.

Caya looked at them and introduced her team-mates to her latest companions. 'Xanor is the closest we have to a team leader and controls Fire. Haero is the youngest of our group, again, a Fire Wielder. Iano and Barek both work Earth and act like twins a lot of the time. They aren't actually related, save through race. Nesqo manipulates Air and has been working with Scortia, my sister.' She smiled, looking between the two groups. 'Have I missed anything?'

They all shook their heads and returned to their own conversations, catching up on all they had missed. The rest of Qwenox, however, did share uneasy looks towards the Dracona. They knew the stories and wondered why one would help their cause. It was not until Caya told them the full story that they finally smiled to Amerita, understanding.

Mattias turned away from the group to talk privately with Xophîn.

~*How are the walls holding?*~ he asked, his voice marred by a hint of guilt, guilt for not being able to help Vantrörkî sooner.

~*They are holding well, for now. You have plenty of time still, my friend. Do not fear. Should our situation worsen, you will be alerted,*~ the Vertex replied with a smile.

~*I would rather we could come to your aid this instant, but we never finished our business in Dra'noxia.*~

~*Then finish it. If you do not, you will not feel free to help anyone. You have time. We have time. It may be shorter than we would prefer, but it is still there. Take what time you have.*~

Mattias sighed and nodded, glancing at his growing group of companions. ~*Very well. We will call on you again when we arrive, should we not need you before.*~

Xophîn nodded sadly, studying the boy's face. ~*I know the thought has already crossed your mind a number of* times, but I will voice it anyway: you have had to grow up far too soon. I am sorry you have had to miss out on the joys of childhood. If only another could shoulder this burden, for you should be having fun at your age, not saving realms.~

~It was partly through our own choice. We could have walked away from our destiny. But I am glad no other shoulders this fate. The guilt would be enough if I knew that I had caused another to bear this burden.~

~Spoken as the true son of Scarien. We will all miss your father, but he has left a fine son to lead us all from disaster. Travel safe, Mattias. I wish you luck.~ He nodded gently and signalled to Vlökir. ~Until we meet again,~ he called as he melted into the shadows.

Vlökir rolled his eyes slightly and waved his own farewell, following his father. The group were left standing on the surface, Qwenox still deep in discussion.

Amerita smiled gently. 'It is time that I, too, took my leave of you. Good luck, to all of you,' she said loudly so as to alert the team to her leaving. Smiling to Mattias and Camer, she opened a Gate back to Drazdéré, leaving the adolescents alone on Havern.

~Well,~ Mattias began, after a long silence, ~we're finally all together.~

Scortia nodded, looking back down into the vast Valley. ~So, where to now?~

~Cyphia. We have to go back to Dra'noxia. We still have business there that we never got to finish,~ Mattias replied before handing her the letter from their father. *~Read this. Our father would have wanted you to.~*

As she read, Camer glanced at Mattias's watch. *~If this is keeping time for once, we should rest here and move in the morning. We don't want to risk entering Cyphia during a shift change.~*

Mattias looked at it and nodded. *~We would be pushing it and we may not be able to find cover.~*

The others nodded and they searched for an empty cave in which to spend the night. The place they found was warm and dry and would shelter them all.

Mattias smiled faintly, watching the sun set over the land, sending streams of green across the sky. *~We should watch in pairs. Two hours each.~* He settled at the cave entrance, watching the sky, his thoughts elsewhere.

Haero walked over to him, curious. *~What's the matter?~* he asked. The young boy felt some sort of connection to Mattias, the pair both being Elementalists of Fire.

Mattias continued to watch the sky, not meeting the boy's gaze. *~Too much. You would not understand.~*

~I'm not just a kid, so don't treat me as one. Try me.~

Mattias looked at him. *~What is it like to be a child*

without responsibility or any real care for the world beyond their own?~

~You know. Everyone tells you what to do and no one listens to you. You can do anything you want really. You know.~ he shrugged lightly. ~So what's wrong?~

~It's nothing.~ He sighed slightly, falling silent and blocking out his thoughts.

But Haero would not let the matter drop, so Xanor quickly intervened, laying a hand on his shoulder.

~Leave him, Haero. You wouldn't understand,~ he said, leading the child away.

~You all always say that. I might understand. You don't know.~

~In this case, you wouldn't. Trust me.~

Mattias turned his gaze to the horizon, the evening breeze light on his face. The past few days had held so much. Too much had happened in such a short space of time. He just needed time to think, alone. He needed to order his thoughts. He had to be able to be strong for the others. They could not possibly understand.

Camer walked over and settled beside him. ~How are you holding up?~ he asked, guessing, in part, his friend's mind.

Mattias shrugged, not really having an answer to that. He was not sure of how he was doing himself.

Camer nodded and watched the land beyond the cave. *~It's beautiful. I always wanted to see the other realms. I never knew I would, or under such circumstances.~*

~Yes. Beautiful indeed, but it holds a dark secret.~ Mattias smiled. *~I sound like a Cloran. Cryptic.~*

Camer could not help but laugh slightly. *~It could be worse.~*

~It is a shame that the beauty will be wiped from worlds such as these, unless we can succeed.~

~We can,~ Camer said bluntly, thinking. *~We just don't know how yet.~*

~The odds are against us, Camer. We know not how nor when to use our powers. How can we possibly heal the realms without the means to do so.~

~We will find the means. I am confident that we will.~ He smiled at his friend. *~Now that we are all together here, maybe it is time.~*

Mattias looked blankly at him for a moment before realising what he meant. *~Are you sure?~* he asked, frowning slightly. *~It seems a little hasty to me.~*

Camer shrugged and looked into the cave at the group settling down. *~It feels right. Besides, if not now, then when. Will there be another chance for us?~*

Mattias nodded, sighing slightly. *~When they are all asleep, we'll wake the girls.~*

Darkness

Night fell slowly, the greens fading out to deep blues and purples, forming the swirling pattern of the night sky. The ground was cloaked in shadow, seeming black in contrast to the lighter sky. Qwenox eventually managed to fall asleep, the excitement of seeing each other again tiring them.

Mattias and Camer looked at each other, silently scanning the group for any sign of alertness. Finding none, they moved carefully and quietly to each of the girls.

They woke them gently, quickly keeping them both from crying out to the others.

~*Quiet. Come outside. There is something we need to do,*~ Mattias told them before making his way out into the crisp night air.

Together, they made their way to a flat stretch of land, large enough for them to spread out. Mattias pulled out the Zynoran, carefully unwrapping it.

~*We need to swap our inheritance chains. None of us have the ones we should.*~ He unfastened the chain from around his neck, handing the snake inheritance chain to Camer. ~*Earth belongs to you.*~

Camer unfastened the eagle and passed it to Scortia. ~*Air, I believe, is your Element and inheritance.*~

~*Fire for you, Mattias,*~ Caya said with a smile. She gave him the salamander she had been wearing and looked at Scortia.

Scortia frowned slightly. ~*I'm going to miss my seahorse.*~

~*But it is not rightfully yours, Scortia. They were switched to draw us together as each pulls to its rightful owner,*~ Mattias said firmly.

~*I know, but still ... it has brought me a lot of comfort over these past years.*~

Caya hugged her. ~*I know, but surely your own will suit you more. You can fly free like the eagle you hold in your hands.*~

Scortia nodded and undid the clasp on the chain, handing the seahorse to her best friend and twin. ~*Water is yours, and yours alone.*~

They each secured their inheritance chains about their necks, leaving the pendants out over their clothes.

Mattias nodded approvingly. ~*We need to form a circle, equally spaced at each of the quarter marks. The order,*~ he said, studying the order of the Zynoran, ~*is Camer at the first mark, Scortia at the next, working clockwise. Then there's me and finally Caya. Girls opposite girls and boys opposite boys.*~ He watched as they each moved into position, taking up his own.

Unravelling the chains on the Zynoran, he moved into the circle to pass them to their owners, starting with

Caya and working round. ~*This is the last Zynoran, a gift from the Clorans.*~

As his friend took his position, Camer began somehow knowing the words he had to say. He firmly held the chain connecting him to Earth. ~*I come here with loyalty in my heart. As Earth I provide the foundation, and I hereby claim my Inheritance.*~

The others watched as three bands of light, carrying the colours of Earth, burst from the Zynoran, snaking up the chain to wind around his hands; green, brown and gold.

Scortia bit her lip before continuing. ~*I come here, with peace in my heart. As Air I breathe life and spirit, and I hereby claim my Inheritance.*~

Again, three bands of light coiled about her hands, this time carrying the pastel colours of Air; yellow and purple and silver.

Mattias smiled at the others, saying his part confidently. ~*I come here with passion in my heart. As Fire I burn brightly to lead the way, and I hereby claim my Inheritance.*~

Mattias's bonds were brightly coloured with red, orange, and gold.

~*I come here with love in my heart. As Water I give clarity to find the way, and I hereby claim my Inheritance,*~

Caya said, her hands quickly encircled with blue, cyan and silver lights.

They all looked at each other, barely having a moment before being lifted up into the air, standing on platforms of their elemental colours, each colour crisscrossing inside the circle below them.

Together, they spoke, to seal their connection and complete the breaking of the Zynoran. *~We all are here, in perfect trust, to protect the balance and heal the realms. Together we stand, never alone. This is our right and our duty. Together, we embrace our destiny and claim our parts of the Zynoran.~*

The four symbols on each piece of the Zynoran were projected into the air, glowing brightly high above them. These phantom copies continued to rise, slowing down before falling outwards towards each child. Before they could turn away, the symbols were burned into their foreheads and the light faded, dropping them gently back to Earth. As they fell, the Zynoran broke in four, each positioning itself around its owner's neck, sealing closed.

The inheritance chains melted away, the pendants each merging with the piece of Zynoran, changing in colour to match the Element. The first part of the Prophecy had been fulfilled.

Power.
A burst of power.
Surging through.
The Void is buzzing.

Something has happened.
Destiny has been awoken.
What will come forth?

What does this mean…

…for me?

Chapter 8

As the Dragon flies

The four quickly regained their senses, standing up. Almost simultaneously, they lifted their hands to their foreheads. The skin there was almost smooth, but they could just about feel the outline of the symbols.

They looked around, the night unchanged by their activities, everything peaceful as it had been before.

Qyan was awake and awaiting their return. As they walked into the cave he looked up from his seat. He smiled and motioned for them to join him. Reaching into his pack, he pulled out a small bowl and set it beside him.

Mattias watched curiously as he built a small fire, lighting it without the aid of magick. *~I can help you with that if you wish.~*

~No. There is something to be enjoyed when a task is completed in a more difficult manner,~ he replied, heating the

bowl over the flames, the powder within becoming a creamy liquid in seconds. *~You will need this. To cover up those marks. Otherwise all will know who you are and you will endanger yourself.~* He dabbed a small amount onto Caya's forehead, carefully blending it in. Indeed, it covered the symbol completely and invisibly. It was as if nothing had ever touched her forehead. He looked at the others, their own symbols shining brightly in the firelight. *~This will shield them from watchful eyes and will not wash off. There is a solution that can remove it should you wish, but nothing else will.~*

They each took their turn to have their foreheads covered, the symbols hidden in an instant and the lotion blending immediately to their own skin.

Stowing the bowl away carefully, Qyan smiled again and motioned to four sleeping areas he had set up for them. *~I will take the next watch. You need to rest after your act tonight. You will find, come morning, that it has drained you more than you realise.~*

Gratefully, they nodded, settling down for the night, Qyan remaining at the entrance to keep watch. His eyes on the landscape, he quietly extinguished the fire, sensing the eyes that had been watching all night. It was those eyes that had awoken him.

Darkness

* * * * * * * * * * * *

As the sun rose, Qyan awoke the sleepers, having kept watch the whole night. He was still recovering from his separation, but he had used the time to reform some of the mental connections.

~*Quickly, the Havern are searching. They have been all night.*~ He paused, frowning. ~*They are getting close.*~

Caya frowned at him, studying his face. ~*Have you been watching all night?*~ she asked accusingly.

~*I could not sleep, so best to allow the others rest. Besides, it does not matter now. Shall we leave before we are discovered?*~

Mattias watched out from the entrance, his belongings already packed away. ~*Does anyone know what they actually want?*~

~*They threw us in a cell! They attacked us!*~ Nesqo exclaimed, ~*I am sure that whatever they want cannot be good for us?*~

~*We may consider that as showing cruel intentions. But what if, to them, they were treating you to their luxuries?*~ Mattias mused.

Camer picked up the train of thought, understanding his friend's reasoning. ~*We know nothing of their customs. Maybe we should ask them. From a distance, of course,*~ he said, the last sentence spoken quickly in response to the incredulous faces around him.

After some more discussion, it was decided. They had come to the conclusion quickly, but despite some dissatisfaction, they had all agreed. Caya would be holding open a Gate while Mattias spoke to the Havern. The others would be working together to create a shield, strong enough to keep the Havern out.

Once everything had been organised, the dome-shaped shield was raised, extending out far enough to allow Mattias to leave the cave safely. From inside, they could see the Havern flocking to the construct, hundreds of black marks on an otherwise clear sky.

Mattias smiled faintly at the others and nodded, stepping out beyond the cave's mouth. He was careful not to go beyond the shield, watching the Havern carefully. Their seemingly frail wings hummed in the silence of the realm.

'What do you want with us?' he shouted, to ensure he was heard over the sound. 'Why did you hold my friends against their will in such deplorable conditions?'

One of the Havern flew down until he was eye to eye with the boy. He hissed like an angry cat, not even testing the shield. 'You insult our hospitality? The room in question has been used by many ... *guests* ... in the past.'

'They were guarded and threatened. Do you call that hospitality? You abducted them.'

'The Havern in question merely lost his temper a little. It is easy to lose control when provoked. Our race can be volatile.

'That does not explain kidnap? What right had you to take them from their home?' he asked angrily, the team silently providing the information.

'We were desperate,' the Havern said, his voice much softer than before. He dropped down to the ground. 'The realm is crumbling through no fault of our own. We thought you could help. We had to find a way to bring you all here.'

'You could have asked.'

The Havern hung his head, hiding the glint in his eye. Mattias looked at the others and frowned, stepping closer, still within the shield.

'We may have an idea as to what is happening, but to save your realm we must first save another.' His frown deepened and he fell silent, startled by the hungry look in the man's eyes.

The Havern reached towards the shield, shattering it in an instant. He gripped Mattias firmly and pulled the boy towards him with startling force. 'You really fell for it.

Every word. Do you not know who we are? We are the pure race. Our hive is legendary. We become stronger ... by consuming other races, absorbing their strength.'

Mattias instantly covered his body in flames, trying to burn the Havern off of him. His grip was spiky and dug into his skin. The others raised their own Elements, trying to help.

'Attack all you want, little Elementalists. It will do nothing to us. You know nothing of the Havern.' He laughed cruelly, drawing a large knife. 'Fast or slow?' he wondered aloud. 'Slow keeps the meat soft.'

He moved quickly, extending Mattias's arm out and sweeping the knife down it. The cut was very deep, running down from his shoulder to his wrist.

The boy cried out in pain, blood flooding out of the wound. The Havern around laughed at his pain, relishing it. The scent of blood was now on the air and they were hungry.

All of a sudden, the skies were clear again, the Havern fleeing in terror. A flock of blue Dragons swooped down, chasing those that remained away.

Two Dragons landed by Mattias, carefully examining the boy.

~Hold on, young one. Now is not your time,~ a majestic

silver Dragon said gently before turning his head to the others. ~*Climb up as we land. We can each carry two of you. Tæmî wishes to speak with you*~

More Dragons landed, surrounding the cave. Grateful for the help, the children mounted quickly. Mattias was then lifted gently by another Dragon and was held safely in his talons as they shot into the air. The rest of the flock joined them and as a single body, they flew eastwards.

After a while, Caya realised that they were no longer on Haveen. Confused she asked the Dragon she was riding, ~*When did we pass from one realm to the next? There was no Gate for us to fly through.*~

~*As Dragons, we need no Gates,*~ came the powerful reply. ~*We have our own means of travel.*~

Caya smiled at the cryptic reply, the old legends came to mind. She remembered stories of their wisdom, but their reluctance to divulge it. They were more inclined to hint at the truth and allow the asker to discover the answers themselves.

~*If you don't mind me asking, who exactly are the Dragons? Everyone knows of them but there are so many stories and nothing is clearly known.*~

Beneath her, she could feel his rumbling laughter; a deep throaty laugh shaking his whole body.

~And with any luck it will remain that way. It is the way we choose to keep it. Very few know us, for knowing a being is to have the power to destroy it. Even Tæmî does not know us. She can simply find us and contact us. We work closely with the Circle, as we deem it to be in the interest of maintaining balance.~ He turned his head slightly to look at her, ever flying straight. ~We come from beyond the realms. No Gate can ever open in our homeland, for we never use them. We are the Guardians, keeping safe the realms we forged.~ He smiled toothily, turning his head back to look on ahead.

~Are you related in any way to the Dracona?~

~Yes and no. Somewhere back beyond all measurement of time a group broke away, preferring our humanoid form. Now, however, we are separate races. They evolved, we did not. However, we are more closely related to the Children of Destiny. Not by blood, but in essence. Only the right souls can ever take on your roles. Your minds will come to function in a similar way to ours as you mature, and you possess many other powers beyond the Elementalists' limitations.~

~How will we know them?~

~Time and patience. When the time is right they will be revealed to you.~

The Dragon never seemed to tire of Caya's inquisitiveness, answering her questions as they came, some openly, but others cryptically. Sometimes he went so far as to steer her from the question itself. While she noticed this, he created more questions in her mind and so she chose not to pursue them. After all, he could have chosen not to answer any of her questions.

After a while, the Dragons dove towards the ground, heading towards the palace below them. Although the dive was frighteningly steep, each landed elegantly, including the one bearing Mattias, despite the fact he had only three feet to land with. Waiting for them were four men bearing a stretcher. They carefully helped transfer the injured boy to the stretcher and lifted it, waiting for the other children to dismount and follow them.

The Dragons bade them farewell in one voice before darting back up into the skies. Within seconds they were gone, presumably having moved into another realm.

The children looked at each other, unsure of what to do next.

'Please, follow us. Tæmî has been waiting for you,' one of the men said softly before they lifted the stretcher between them, walking into the palace.

The walls of the palace were pure silver, gold serving as decoration. The red sunset was reflected brightly, casting a coppery sheen onto the grass surrounding the building. Inside, the walls were lined with gemstones, entire rooms glistening with only one colour. Even the ceiling was covered spectacularly. The floor itself was of a material similar to glass, shielding intricate tapestries from being trampled, the edges marked by white gold to seal the join by each wall. It was instantly clear that Tæmî had expensive tastes, and she clearly would not settle for second best. Nothing seemed out of place.

The Healing room was pure white, white pearls on the walls with marble flooring. Once the children had recovered from the brightness of the room, they found it was a nice room to stay in. It had a calm and soothing atmosphere.

As Mattias was lowered carefully onto a bed, the youths were ushered out to allow the Healers to start their work. Two guards had materialised outside the room and led them away.

They passed through many corridors and past many luxurious rooms before coming to a stop before a large set of double doors. It was made, like all others, from the finest wood, rich in colour. Unlike the rest, however, it was laced with gold lines forming an inverted gold tree. A strange inscription was written above the doors to finish. In addition to that, wherever the branches reached the edge of the doors, they became silver, continuing across the walls and floor, showing the tree's immensity.

The doors were pushed open slowly to reveal the hall beyond. Tæmî sat proud and erect on her throne.

She was a slim young woman with mousy-blond, sleek hair lying lightly over her shoulders. She had a tired, yet beautiful face, marked by only the faintest lines. Her eyes were stunningly blue and were the only feature to truly show her age. In contrast to her youthful appearance, her eyes told of countless years passing them by.

As soon as she saw the children, the worry left her face and she stood quickly, walking down to them.

'So long have I waited, and so long have you been needed. Each of you are most welcome in my halls. These are hard times indeed. Children should never be sent abroad unattended, let alone out into other realms. But then again, I suppose these are far from normal times. I presume Scarien has his reasons for not accompanying you on your journey.'

She looked questioningly at them and Caya and Scortia turned their gaze to Camer, knowing it was his right to answer her on this matter. He hung his head at first, trying to fit the words together.

'Scarien is...' he began eventually, lifting his head once more to look the empress in her eyes. 'He is ... he was taken. He broke his Oath.' He hoped she understood what he meant as he could not find the strength to tell her that the man had died. After all, there was still part of him which refused to believe it. The pain was still too fresh, alongside the memory of that night.

Tæmî closed her eyes, taking in his words and sparing a moment for grief. She had indeed been close to Scarien many years ago. He had touched everyone he worked with in different ways. Even now, despite their long separation, she considered him a close friend. 'He must have meant a lot to both you and Mattias. While we were in contact, he spoke often of you. The Circle owes him much, and on their behalf, I will do all I can to help you. That is what Scarien would have wanted.'

Camer just nodded, not able to say much more than he already had.

She smiled gently at him. 'Come. You must all be exhausted, but first, we must eat. It will get your strength up again.'

She walked through them and the great doors, leading them all to the dining hall. A feast had been set out ready for them towards the head of the table. Each long side held thirteen seats with a seat at either end. Of all these seats, however, only eleven has been set, including

Tæmî's. As they watched, however, one of these places was cleared away to account for Mattias's absence, and instead a candle was placed there.

Note to readers:
The lighting of a candle to mark an absence is by no means unique to Cyphia. It has cropped up in many cultures in many realms to show respect for a missing person.
By marking their place with a candle, it also symbolises that the person is there in spirit and is not forgotten.
To resume:

Tæmî indicated that they should sit and slid gracefully onto her seat at the head of the table. The children followed her lead and she smiled, motioning to the servants around that they could leave. She then gestured towards the food.

'Please. Eat.'

They all plated up some food, and began to eat. Most of them realised just how hungry they were after their ordeal. As they ate, Tæmî spoke with the boys from Qwenox, who were all seated nearest her. Their conversation seemed somewhat muffled to Caya and Scortia, who were sat farthest away.

Camer had scarcely touched his food. For the sake of

politeness, he had taken some food onto his plate, but not feeling hungry, he continuously moved it around. He had far too much on his mind. Caya laid a comforting hand on his shoulder and he looked up from his food. Her plate, he noticed, along with Scortia's, was also untouched.

~We are connected deeply, Camer. We can feel it also. His pain runs along our bond. It is our pain,~ she said silently.

Camer nodded. *~I know. Every time I look at my arm, I expect it to be pouring with blood. I can feel the wound, even if I cannot see it.~*

Scortia lay her fork down, looking at him intently. *~You would be wise to pay close attention to that. Your bond with him will be deeper than ours. Caya suffered injuries on Mount Zircon. At first, I only felt the pain, but then I also gained the same injuries. They developed over time.~* She exchanged a glance with her twin before returning her gaze to Camer. *~Maybe we are linked in our pairs as well as a whole group. The pairings are stronger. Please, hold out your arm.~*

Camer nodded and did as she asked, wincing slightly as the muscle seemed to stretch. Caya's eyes widened slightly and he, himself, could hardly believe what he was seeing, even though he could feel it. On what had previously been smooth skin, a faint scar line travelled down to just below his wrist. Even as they watched, it slowly developed, becoming more prominent and ropy.

Caya gently pressed her fingers over it and Camer bit back a cry, thinking it would burst open with the level of pain. The area was becoming increasingly tender.

~*It appears to be healing backwards, and it's getting faster,*~ said Caya, looking both horrified and fascinated.

~*I don't care what it looks like. It hurts!*~

Camer hid his arm under the table once more as the scar became a scab that itched agonisingly. He was trying to think of an excuse to leave the table and get outside, but was spared the trouble; Tæmî had realised just how little the three had eaten.

'You're worried and beyond tired. A bad combination when you are trying to eat. I can scarcely imagine what must be going through your minds right now. Trust me when I say that your companion is in the very best hands, but the Healers will not allow you in to see him until he is well again.' She smiled gently and clapped her hands, two guards entering. 'You may retire should you wish. The guards will show you which way you must go. I will see you in the morning.'

The three thanked her and rose, quickly leaving the table, the girls helping shield Camer's arm from view, but discretely so. The guards bowed to their empress before leaving the room with the children, leading them down the corridors once more.

They had not left a moment too soon. Only a few minutes later, while walking down an overdone corridor, Camer felt a trickle of blood run down his arm, spreading across the lines on his palm. It partly dried there, making his hand feel sticky. Hoping that not much more would follow, he focussed on getting somewhere safe. However, he could already feel another drop worm its way down his arm.

The pain that had been a dull throb before suddenly changed. There was a searing pain in his arm as though a strip of white-hot metal had been pressed down onto it. He bit his tongue to keep his silence, warm blood trickling down his throat.

As they crossed the courtyard to get to the guest rooms, an emerald-green Dragon landed in front of them.

~*The Dragons have something of great importance to show the Guardian of Earth,*~ he said, his voice deep and rumbling. ~*Come with me, Guardian of Earth.*~

~*He's injured. You can't expect us to let you take him alone,*~ Scortia exclaimed.

~*The others will be shown when it is their time. This is not it. He must come alone.*~ He looked at Scortia and Caya intensely, his statement and expression silencing their questions.

The guards looked at one another as though they

were going to say something, but apparently thought better of it. Nodding to the Dragon, they turned and pointed the girls to the guest rooms.

'Take your pick of whichever room you wish. They are all at your disposal,' one of the pair said before walking off once more, back towards the dining hall.

The three watched them go and then Camer nodded. ~*I'll come,*~ he said, moving to the Dragon's side. ~*Don't worry, you two. I'll be fine.*~ he smiled slightly towards them.

The Dragon crouched down as low as possible, allowing him to climb up easily onto his back. Once the boy was settled, he rose again, preparing for flight.

~*Look after him,*~ Scortia instructed the Dragon. ~*Their bond runs deep and Mattias's wound is appearing on him. You may not have long before he is as badly injured as our brother.*~

The Dragon bowed his head in acknowledgement. ~*I will do my best,*~ he said sincerely before leaping into the air, his great wings unfurling. Their massive strokes took them higher and higher, and it was not long before the realm of Cyphia was far below.

After several long minutes of flying, Camer looked around, asking, ~*Where is it we are going?*~

The Dragon chuckled. ~*Patience, young one. You will find out when we arrive. To tell you so soon would spoil a mystery that is yours to solve.~*

Camer absently rubbed his arm, his hand coming away wet and sticky. He instantly knew that whatever he asked on the subject, the Dragon would not tell him until the right moment. Instead, he asked one of the other questions that had surfaced in his mind. *~What exactly are the Dragons?~*

~Do you not know tales of the Dragons? They should be plentiful among your people. They always have been.~

~We do. Have tales, that is. But that doesn't mean we know what the Dragons are. To most they are just a legend. A mystery. The stories involve the Dragons, they say nothing as to what they are or where they are from.~

~So many forget that legends are based on truths lost to the ravages of time. Nothing is merely a legend. A legend is a play on the truth. One day, you, too, may become a legend. The reality lost in the retellings of your deeds to come. People will view you differently in the times to come,~ the Dragon said, a smile in his voice.

~As for your question, the Dragons are, to some extent, the Guardians of the realms. In the same way that you and your companions are the Guardians of the Elements. In the beginning, the River of Existence and the Void of Nothingness appeared. No one knows why or how, but from them, Kaisha and Rectys, of Life and Death respectively. They were followed by the four

Great Ones of the Elements.~

~Yes, I know that. We are taught that from a young age. Trya, Drôn, Nårio and Berak.~

~Correct. Anyway, together they formed our realm and then all others and gave them all they needed for life to thrive. They looked at what they had achieved and sought to protect it, watch over those that came to live. The race of the Dragons were born of their first dance.~

Camer listened closely, thinking of what he had just heard. It all seemed a lot to take in. He knew of the creation of the realms. All the proof needed existed. Very few doubted it, and they were often mad. Not many would listen to them.

~Do not worry, young one. In time you will gain the ability to use that which we cannot. You will harness wild magick, and save the realms, healing them. You may even have a chance to restore those lost. It is our belief that all Guardians will work together to keep the people safe.

~You will all develop Dragonskills as and when the need is there. Your minds are like those of the Dragons, and only similar minds can take up your role should one of you fall. You share more with us than any other race, even the Dracona.~

The Dragon fell silent, his wings rising and falling steadily on each side. The beat created very slight disturbance in the otherwise still night air.

Suddenly, Camer became aware of having passed into another realm. Looking down and around, he could not see any difference and the air felt the same as it had before. He could just feel something inside telling him they had passed through. Just before the feeling, he remembered seeing a slight shimmer around them, but he had put it down to his tiredness. Now, however, he realised that it had been a Wall, the shimmer caused by the Void surrounding the realms.

~*You say that we will develop Dragonskills, but how will we know how, or when, to use them?*~

~*Most will be instinctive, and will manifest from you, unbidden in response to your situation. Those that are not, however, will be taught to you. We will train you all to realise when your skills are developing.*~

Silence passed between them as Camer got his head around the Dragon's words. He had so many questions, but the answers he was receiving were too deep to process quickly enough.

A few moments later, the curious boy asked yet another question. ~*Do all Dragons breathe fire?*~

The Dragon chuckled and shook his magnificent head. ~*The Dragons are bound the same way that the Elementalists are. Only the Dragons of Fire and all Gold Dragons can use the Flame Breath. Those of Water have the Ice*

Breath, while Air has the Sonic Breath. Silver Dragons can use both of those. As for Earth, we have the Gargoyle breath, again, alongside the Gold Dragons.~ The Dragon paused, as if reluctant to finish. *~And all Dragons have the Death Breath and the Touch of Life. These are by no means all the Dragonskills, however.~*

Camer tilted his head slightly. *~Are the colours of the Dragons dependant on their Element?~*

~Yes, and are also dependant on the form of Element; mutable, cardinal or fixed. You may learn more in time, but for now, we are almost at our destination.~

Camer looked down on the realm below. The ground was cloaked in darkness. He could barely see several large moving shapes. Even from the distance and despite the gloom, he instantly recognised them as more Dragons. At first, he could only see a small number, but as he scanned the ground and skies, he realised just how many there were around them. It was instantly obvious; they were in the realm of the Dragons.

Descendants.
Why do you scorn me so?
Why must you flee?

You work against me.
All we created.

'And so the creation shall turn
on its creator.

And all will fall to ruin.

Chapter 9

The Scent of Death

Lee dusted his hands down on his clothes and picked up a bottle of water. He drank deeply, his work being thirst-inducing. His shift had actually ended two hours previously, but he enjoyed the work. It was challenging and took his mind off many other worries.

As he returned to work, he felt the eyes of another watching him, causing the hairs on his neck to rise. He ignored the sensation, however, carefully heating the metal he was going to work.

'You know, as a Cloran, you needn't heat that. Or do much in the way of work either.'

Lee turned, holding the metal steady in the furnace. By the workbench stood one of the camp's senior officers. Lee adjusted his hold on the metal to prevent it falling into the heat and saluted carefully, ever keeping half an eye of the temperature of the metal he was heating. He did not wish to lose any of it to the flames.

The officer returned the salute and approached the boy. 'So why don't you?' he asked curiously. 'You would save a lot of time and effort.

Lee removed the glowing shard from the heat and lay it flat and began to hammer it into shape. When he finally chose to speak, he raised his voice to make his answer clear. 'I might have done so once, when I was younger. But I've changed. What would I achieve by using my abilities to shape any piece of metal I am given. Perfection isn't all I want. By working hard to achieve the result, a higher level of satisfaction is achieved. There is nothing to be learnt from cheating.'

He brought the hammer down slightly harder than he had intended and cracked the softened metal. He cursed and shouted for Qyesar.

'You wouldn't have such problems,' the officer observed.

'But then I would never learn to fix my mistakes, or avoid them altogether.'

'Well said, Lee,' Qyesar remarked as he strode in. He saluted the officer briefly before inspecting the damage. 'It could be much worse. What do you think you should do?'

'I could try to reforge the join carefully, but that may risk a weakness in the blade. Or I could start over.'

'Only start again if you have to. Trust in your ability to forge this piece of metal. You will do fine. You were already doing well.' Qyesar smiled, proud of the boy. 'Just take care when you try to reforge it. We don't want a blade that has a very thick centre, else it will be off-balance and useless in combat.'

Leaving Lee to try again, he stepped towards the officer. 'Can I help you sir?' he asked.

'It was you I was waiting for. Please, follow me.'

Qyesar turned to Lee. 'Will you be able to hold the fort? I am sure I will not be kept long.'

'Well, that will depend,' the officer interjected softly, something in his voice disturbing the boy.

Lee shrugged, hiding his feeling. 'I'll be fine. I'll call Francin if I need help.' He kept his gaze from the officer, not trusting the man, or his false smile. He returned to his work, heating the area he needed to rejoin until it was red hot and soft enough to work. As he overlapped the pieces and began to hammer again, he saw Qyesar leave with the officer. Something was not right, and he was not going to let anything happen to his friend.

Once he was sure that Qyesar was out of earshot, he called for Francin. The ever-happy and ever-optimistic man came quickly.

'What is it, Lee?'

'Could you finish this for me? I promised to get it done but I have to be somewhere.'

'Of course I can. It won't take me long, mate.'

'Thank you!' Lee called as he ran out of the forge. He was learning to trust his instincts and right now, they told him something was wrong with that officer.

As he darted out of the door, he glimpsed Qyesar turning out of sight. He ran silently to catch up and then followed them discretely, taking care to stay out of sight, should they turn. He frowned slightly. They were heading further and further away from the camp.

Closing his eyes, Lee became hidden from sight, walking invisibly towards the pair. The fields were too open for him to hide in. This way, they could not see him, but his vision was not hampered by some object he was behind. No. He could see them very well.

'Why are we out here, officer?' Lee heard Qyesar ask. But it wasn't for a few seconds before he saw the man's mouth for the words. Cursing silently, he moved behind a tree, becoming visible once more. He needed to see things as they happened.

From where he was, he could barely hear the officer's reply. 'I do not wish to be ... overheard.'

Something's wrong, Lee thought to himself, *He took too long to answer.*

Cautiously, he edged around the tree so that he could see the pair. Luckily for him, neither man noticed him, both of them focussed on the other.

'Very well, officer. I'm listening,' Qyesar said slowly.

He knows. He knows something is wrong here. Lee paused for a moment, noticing something else in Qyesar's voice. *He knows I'm here. He knows I followed.*

'Good. Now listen hard and listen well.' He paused, glancing around carefully. He did not seem to see Lee, but when he continued, the boy had to strain to hear. 'It has come to our attention that Scarien Éscaronôvic has ... moved on. This does not bode well for us. However, *you* were named are the one we should turn to. However, while we trusted Éscaronôvic, we do not know you nor know if we can trust you.'

'What do you mean?' Qyesar asked, suddenly tense and alert.

'You must come with us to Vantrörkî. You will spend time there and we will decide. It has been agreed with the woman now running this camp. The choice is now yours.

You can come and hopefully gain the trust of the Vertex. However, if you refuse ... should we survive our current struggle, then we join with the opposition.'

'And what if you don't? Survive, that is.'

'You needn't worry in that case, for there will be none left to care. Existence will fall.'

'Very well, I will come,' Qyesar said decisively, 'but not straight away. I have a shift to finish and a bag to pack.'

'I shall wait here. You have one hour.'

Qyesar nodded and turned, walking away. The man smiled and sat down under the tree.

Lee grimaced. Even if here were to leave invisibly, there was no way he would manage to go without being heard. The stranger was too close.

An hour. Just an hour, Lee, he thought to himself. But he knew he would scarcely manage to stand that long. He had not sat down since breakfast and he had missed dinner. From where he was, he could just about lean comfortably against the tree, but he could not sit down; it would create too much noise. *Getting here was so easy. If only I could leave just as easily. But I don't know how I could manage it.*

Lee leant carefully against the tree, pausing every time he thought his feet had made a noise. The silence around him made him feel like every movement was amplified into the loudest sound.

The man yawned, stretching out. Lee could see his hands on each side of the tree.

And so they waited. For Lee, it was the longest hour of his life. In that hour he felt the minutes slip by and, with nothing to distract him, they each felt like an hour themselves. He did not dare move to make himself more comfortable, lest he make the slightest sound. But he felt the cramps settle into his muscles, gradually becoming harder to bear.

Ten minutes to the hour, by Lee's count, he could see a man walking towards them from the camp. Qyesar only had a small rucksack. He really understood the principle of 'bare necessities'. Behind him, a woman ran up. Lyana. She embraced him briefly and handing him a letter before walking back to the camp. Before she disappeared from view, she turned and waved a final farewell.

Qyesar resumed his journey, nodding to the man as he drew near. 'I am ready,' he said, watching him nervously.

'Good. Just one more thing before we go...' he reached into a shadow and pulled out a man, almost identical in appearance, but slightly shorter. He muttered something to this newcomer in soft undertones, seemingly in another language. The newcomer nodded and departed.

'This encounter has been watched by another,' the Vertex said softly. Qyesar tensed.

Lee suddenly felt someone grab him from behind. Turning quickly, the other person was standing there. As he started to step back, he was seized.

'Lookee here, Vex. I found me a rat.'

Qyesar started forward. 'Leave him alone. He means no harm,' he said angrily. His anger, however, was not directed at the boy; it was the man restraining him.

'Or what?' the Vertex asked, giving the boy a rough shake. His eyes glowed a faint red.

'Lee,' Qyesar said softly, held back by the first of the two Vertex. 'I give you full permission to hurt him.'

'You hear that, Vex? The kid has permission to hurt me,' the man laughed, holding Lee even tighter. 'What are you gonna do to me, boy?'

'Watch yourself, Xern. Never underestimate those you don't know,' Vex said carefully, releasing Qyesar as he stopped struggling.

Xern laughed, his free arm hooking around Lee's neck. 'Do you know what we do with rats, boy?' He paused, grinning manically. 'No? We kill 'em.'

Vex held Qyesar back again as the man lunged

forwards. Xern's grip tightened about the boy's neck and Lee's eyes widened in panic. His mouth opened as he tried to force air down his throat.

'Lee!' Qyesar shouted, trying to pull free of Vex. 'Let go of me!'

Vex shook his head. 'I do that and Xern will kill him in an instant. He has the Deathscent now. If he cannot regain control himself, or if your boy cannot help himself, then there is no hope. I did not want him here. He is unreliable. Any other Vertex would have been enough.'

Lee saw a black haze creep into his vision. He could not give up. Xern was focussed now on something else, something he could not detect himself, but it weakened the grip Xern had around his body. His arms were free and he reached up, pulling on the arm about his neck. Half a breath crept into his lungs, fuelling him and clearing his vision slightly. However, a persistent ringing in his ears was distracting him. There had to be a way out of this, if only he could think straight...

As the blackness crept in again, he felt his panic levels rising. He could not focus. He was dimly aware of Qyesar, still fighting Vex's grip. His rational thoughts were changing, becoming irrational through desperation. He could feel the heat rising in his body, uncontrolled. He vaguely registered his throat being released suddenly, a rush of air filling his lungs, before he blacked out completely.

Xern released his hold suddenly, burnt. He was about to go again for the boy when Lee collapsed. Realising what he had done, his mind cleared and he stepped back, shaking off the lingering scent. Vex released Qyesar as both men ran forward. Qyesar dropped down beside Lee, slapping his face until he began to come back to the world.

Lee tried to groan, but his throat was far too sore. His vision was hampered by blotchy spots of red. His hands and feet tingled strangely, but the ringing in his ears slowly began to fade.

Vex sat by Xern, comforting the man who was clearly shocked by his own doing. Despite his remorse, Qyesar could feel no sympathy for him; sorry always came too late. However, he did listen to the exchange between the pair, soon coming to understand.

'It wasn't your fault, Xern. There is no reason for you to be unmade. The Deathscent is strong. It takes over.'

'Exactly, it's too strong. I cannot control it. You have a Darkblade. Unmake me,' Xern snapped, turning on his companion.

'No! I will not! I ... I cannot. You may plead your case

to the Clan, but it is unlikely to be heard. You were not one of those who took the 'Scent willingly; it was forced upon you.' Vex looked sad, the expression strange on his black face. 'You have coped better than the others. You have regained a measure of control: you have not killed.'

'Not yet, but I have come so close. I almost did tonight. A child at that. No older than my own. The longer I go, the harder it is. I cannot control it.'

Qyesar watched Xern, inwardly cursing himself for hating the man. He wondered how he must feel, knowing he could risk killing his own child. The man looked devastated, at the end of his tether, like he had no options left. He was not the cold-blooded killer he had seen before, and he strangely felt the need to say something.

'We all do things that we're not proud of. Just because you feel like you fail, does not mean you should give up. It is only through quitting that we truly fail. Take strength from others.'

Xern felt a stab of comfort. 'After what I did, I expected you to hate me, not comfort me. Thank you…'

Qyesar nodded, and Vex smiled gratefully at him. 'If only you would open your eyes and see, we've been trying to help you. You just never let us. You avoided us so much, we never had the chance.'

'You don't know what it's like,' muttered Xern, 'I have always been afraid. Afraid of what I might do.'

With that final comment still fresh in the air, Xern vanished, melting away into the nearest shadow.

Lee shook his head to clear the remaining blotches in his vision and sat up slowly. He paused in the motion, feeling dizzy, but the moment soon passed and he felt almost as good as he had before the incident.

Qyesar helped the boy to his feet and Vex looked intently at them.

'He has to come with us now, after what he has heard this night. It would be better for him anyway.' He smiled, looking as though nothing had happened.

Lee looked pleadingly at Qyesar, desperate to see something new. He had a very good feeling about Vantrörkî. He could see the man caving in.

Qyesar turned to Vex. 'Fine. But if any harm comes to him, I'm holding you personally responsible,' he warned.

'I can accept that. Now come. Take my hand and whatever happens. Do. Not. Let. Go. Not until I tell you too. I am not hunting you down in the Wastelands.'

With Qyesar on his right, and Lee on his left, Vex stepped forwards into a shadow, dragging both of them with him. And suddenly, Catré was gone, dissolved into

Darkness

the darkness.

The Balance.
It moves.
New forces are at work.

The boy.
It is all about the boy.

Chapter 10

Guardian of Earth

Tæmî sighed, the children all having left the table for bed. She had enjoyed the company, but felt troubled. Pushing herself out from the table, she rose from her seat slowly and made her way to the Healers. For the first time, she looked on her long elaborate corridors in disgust as they prolonged her journey unnecessarily. She wondered about her priorities, and what she should do, once this was all over.

As she finally approached the door, she stopped, hesitant. She was apprehensive of what she would find there. What would happen if they had arrived too late? What if…?

She knocked twice. She respected the Healers and it was the only place in her own home she would not enter without permission. She stood outside for an agonising few minutes, listening, but hearing nothing. She was about to turn away when the door cracked open and a man clad in white slipped out.

'How is he?' she asked quickly, trying to get a glimpse inside before the door closed.

The man pressed the door shut behind him, his expression grim. 'It's not looking good. We will know more by the morning. There is more to his injury than we can fathom. For one, we cannot close the wound, nor slow the bleed.'

'Is he going to be alright?'

'We will know more by morning,' the man repeated. His expression softened. 'Now, Empress, please get some rest. You will do him nor us any good by getting yourself ill. You need to keep to your routine.'

'Yes. Of course. I … I apologise. Please, keep me informed.'

'As ever, Empress. Goodnight.'

'Goodnight,' she replied, walking off quickly.

He watched her go before slipping back into the room. 'Someone will need to check on the empress come morning. She is pushing herself again, and this is without the duties of the Circle,' he said as he went back to Mattias.

Darkness

The boy was nearly as white as the walls around, and nothing they could do would close his wound.

* * * * * * * * * * * *

Camer marvelled at the great beings, his grip on the Dragon slackening as he turned to watch them. Their colours were dazzling, harmonising with each other. Every flight seemed like a dance. The varying shades seemed to light up the brightening sky.

He was so captured by their magnificence that he forgot how far he was from the ground. Suddenly, the Dragon he was riding swooped into a dive, jerking him back to the moment. He grabbed on tight, focussed once more. He could not afford to keep his head in the clouds.

Screwing his eyes shut, his grip tightened on the scaly surface. Even though he could not see it, he could still feel the ground hurtling ever closer.

* * * * * * * * * * * *

Far off in another realm, three children jerked awake. Two glanced at each other from across the room they had chosen to share. They silently comforted each other, the feeling of falling fading fast. After only a moment, they both lay down, drifting back to sleep.

The other was surrounded by white and people, also clad in white, quickly forced him back down, muttering an incantation. *Am I dead?* he wondered, but as he opened his mouth to ask, the words would not come. His vision faded once more into blackness.

* * * * * * * * * * * *

Camer only opened his eyes again as he felt the Dragon land, his fear ebbing away quickly. He paused for a moment, regaining his senses before dismounting and carefully dropping to the ground.

The grass was strange beneath his feet. It was unusually springy and each step seemed incredibly light to him. After taking just a few steps, he realised that there was no mark of his passing. Looking around, he realised that even the great Dragons left no sign.

A group of Earth Dragons swooped down from the sky, landing around them. Despite their size and the fact they were designed for the sky, they clearly moved with the same agility and gracefulness on the ground as they did whilst flying, if not more.

~Come with us,~ they all said in unison.

Camer nodded and walked with the group. He knew instantly that they had slowed their usual pace for his sake, but he was still hard pushed to keep from falling behind. If he had been any other normal boy, he would have been exhausted or unconscious, or both. However, due to his power and his life in the Letran camp, he could find the strength he needed. But he could feel the opening scar throb as he moved, each beat of his heart making it more painful.

They travelled for what felt like hours, the pace unwavering. Eventually, however, the Dragons slowed, gradually stopping altogether. All around, Camer could only see the vast, green plains.

'What is it?' Camer asked aloud, confused. There was nothing here.

~We have come as far as we are permitted,~ one of the Dragons replied. ~The one who brought you must take you the next step.~

Camer frowned, but followed the Dragon away from the group. Looking back, he saw them form a vast circle, but he could not understand why. He turned his gaze back to his companion, who was moving more slowly; the boy was tiring. Camer frowned, unable to keep from rubbing the scab. He never scratched it, however, fearful of breaking through the barrier. The itching was intolerable and the pain was growing, becoming sharper.

After a few minutes in silence, the Dragon spoke. *~You feel pain. Yet the pain is not your own,~* he remarked.

Camer nodded. *~Mattias was the one injured.~*

~It is still a grievous wound. Your bond with the Fire Guardian is deeper than you know. You are Four divided into Two. We will visit with you. If left too late, healing will be impossible. Even for us.~

The Dragon fell silent once more, leaving Camer to think about what he had just said. Another few minutes passed before the boy spoke again.

~What is your name?~ he asked curiously.

The Dragon remained silent for several moments more, as though he were weighing his answer carefully. *~A name, Camer Tari, is a very powerful thing to hold. You do not understand what forces bind you to your name. My true name you will never be able to pronounce, nor would I reveal it. However, you may call me Verton.~*

Verton stopped. *~I can take you no further, for this journey must be yours alone. It is not far. Walk slowly and do not look back. Enter the Circle. You will know what to do. I will come when I can.~*

Camer frowned slightly, but nodded, beginning to walk forwards. His legs felt like lead, as though something were dragging him back. *Is this my Destiny? Are ties to the past holding me back?* he pondered. He wanted nothing more than to turn, look back. He wanted to run home and make everything be as it was, before all this. He needed to know that he was not alone. But in this, he was alone. There was no more turning back. He had to keep moving forwards.

Five minutes passed, but felt more like five hours. A great pillar rose up into his line of sight. The Pillar of Earth. He recognised it instantly. Something within him stirred, knowing that he belonged here. The Earth was kin to him. The Pillar held the very essence of the element it represented. Colours rippled down its sides, earth colours, colours of life.

Around the pillar, a large circle was marked out with the same substance, creating a lip. Both pillar and rim shone dimly in the growing gloom. As he approached, Camer could see that between the rim and the pillar itself was a vast Nothing, broken only by three spokes of different colours. *Mutable. Cardinal. Fixed,* his heart said.

Note to readers:

For those of you not the least bit into astrology, it is important that you know which signs constitute to Mutable, Cardinal and Fixed signs.

All the original Children of Destiny *are Cardinal signs: the Ram, the Crab, the Scales and the Sea-goat. The second generation are of Fixed signs: the Bull, the Lion, the Scorpion and the Water Carrier. Finally, the signs left are Mutable, and are made up of the Twins, the Virgin, the Archer and the Two Fish.*

The powers each child holds will be related to the properties of their sign. Also, other important details come to light as a result of this information.

Read carefully, for something is amiss if all I have said is true.

To resume:

Suddenly Camer knew what he had to do. Approaching cautiously, he stood at the edge of one of the spokes. Reaching into it with his mind, he shook his head.

'Cardinal,' he muttered, moving clockwise to the next one. 'Mutable,' he said, repeating the procedure, for it, too, was not right.

It had to be the last one. He was born into Earth under the sign of the Bull. His path was Fixed, and the only one he could ever walk upon. Moving to the final spoke, he stepped onto the thin beam, balancing carefully so that he did not fall into Nothing. However, he need not have feared, for he seemed to be stuck to the spoke. He could walk along it, but his feet were drawn back to it constantly. The colours rippled along it as he walked, as if he were walking over still water. The ripples, when they reached the pillar, moved up it in waves.

Watching his feet, he stepped slowly but surely towards the centre, the Nothing pressing in all around him, threatening to pull him off, and coaxing him to jump.

Camer ignored it, focussing on the colours rippling underneath him. It was only a few more steps to the pillar. He was so close, he could not even feel his arm throbbing, despite the wound opening fully.

Once he reached the end of the spoke, he realised that there was a gap between his feet and the pillar. He knew he could not leave the beam beneath his feet, so he reached out towards the pillar. It was just out of reach, but he stretched further with his blood-stained hand, eventually managing to press his palm against the pillar. Slowly, it accepted his hand, allowing it to sink just below the surface, connecting him to the essence of Earth itself.

A massive surge of energy rushed through him, threatening to dislodge him. However, he seemed to be glued to the structure. His mind filling with the power that the pillar had to offer him. Everything was here that he would ever need to carry out his duty as Guardian.

Guardian of Earth. He could see the raw energy. He could see right into the essence of indescribable beauty and horror, kindness and malice, into the reaches of life and death.

And suddenly, it was over, the pillar returning to normal for barely an instant before vanishing altogether. The spokes withdrew into the rim, leaving Camer lying on the outside of the Circle with no idea how he got there. The Circle remained, a pit of nothing contained by a small rim of Earth, just enough to keep it contained. Camer was now the Pillar of Earth until his purpose was complete.

Dazed, shaken and badly bleeding was how Verton found the boy. Gently, he lifted Camer in his talons and took flight, heading for Cyphia.

Earth.
The first of the Four.
I can feel it.
The power grows.

So, the beginning will soon be over.
Soon.

Soon…

Chapter 11

Gathering

The sensation Lee felt as they passed from Light to Shadow almost knocked him off his feet. He only remained standing due to Vex's strong grip. The feeling had come suddenly and without warning, but it had passed in the same instant. Lee grimaced, feeling like a glass of water being drunk.

Once they were through, Qyesar moved to release Vex's hand, but the Vertex maintained a strong grip.

~Not yet. If you let go, you'll go straight to the Wasteland, and I, for one, will not be travelling there to find you. I must take you to the Clan.~

They walked quickly, but not so fast that Lee fell behind, through the Outskirts. A great city was barely visible in the distance. Vex had told them, as they walked, that they would continue in this manner towards the City unless they heard the Call. If it sounded once, they would continue as they were, twice and they would run and three times…

'Let us hope that it does not sound three times,' he said, not feeling the need to expand on that at all.

Vex lead them confidently through the Outskirts, keeping them away from any dangers. Every time Qyesar tried to ask what the Call was, he got no answer.

Despite the pace they were walking at, the city drew no nearer. It remained fixed firmly in the distance, and yet they continued to move on, only ever pausing briefly to catch their breath.

Lee quickly found that keeping track of time was impossible on Vantrörkî. He could not clearly see his watch due to the gloom and the level of light was constant; there was no way of measuring time. But then it must be said, the shadows had no need for time in their own world, and they were always acutely aware of the passing of time in all other worlds.

After what could have been five days, or possibly longer, the city was finally starting to seem much closer, the buildings stretching up and disappearing into the half-light. However, despite the considerable length of time, Lee and Qyesar barely felt hungry, as though it had only been a matter of minutes since they had left their home behind.

Darkness

Around the buildings, they could see dark shadows flitted about their business, paying no attention to the three Travellers. After all, any important matters would be discussed at the next Gathering, and the trio were still far away.

Even as Qyesar watched, all those shadows vanished, a long sounding cry resounding through Vantrörkî. It was the sound of pure darkness, ringing through the minds of every Vertex in every realm, calling them home. All around them, the air was filled with moving Darkness as Shadows went home.

Vex halted, listening intently. 'Do you hear that?' he asked the pair.

Qyesar shook his head, sensing something different, but hearing nothing. Lee, however, had frozen, his eyes rolling back in his head. His grip tightened on Vex's hand and would have broken it were the man not made of Shadow.

Acting quickly, Vex murmured a spell of sleep, bending so that the boy fell over his shoulders as he slumped. Throughout this manoeuvre, he never released Qyesar's hand.

The Call had faded again into nothing, but Vex looked worriedly into Qyesar's eyes. 'For his sake, we must run.'

They ran through the streets of the deserted city, ever gaining speed. Vex led Qyesar to the wall of one particular building. None of the structures had windows or doors and Qyesar wondered how they would get in.

However, Vex stood right in front of it and spoke. 'Vexon Narønya, responding to the Call, mark 8. I bring two guests who represent the Letrans, breakaway group of the Nameless. Request urgent assistance for one injured.'

There was a long silence before a voice hissed, 'Enter.'

Qyesar was about to ask how they were supposed to do that when Vex pulled him through the wall. Almost as soon as he was through, a black band was clamped around his wrist. Vex let go of his hand and moved so that the process could be repeated on Lee.

'Follow us,' one of the men said, his voice as soft and subtle as the dusk

They were led to a great, round hall, half-full as the Vertex gathered, and getting fuller as they moved.

'When everyone has arrived, every seat is full and there are one hundred standees around the wall,' Vex muttered to Qyesar. 'If even one person is unaccounted for, searches are sent out and the Gathering will not begin until they are found. There has not been a problem for over fifteen thousand cycles.'

Carefully, he lay Lee on a table, rousing him with a single word. He turned to the man still behind him. 'He heard the Call. He is one of the Vanished.'

The man nodded, stepping forwards to examine the boy. 'He is not of any relation?'

'No. The effect was unexpected.'

Lee's eyes opened, the whites of his eyes still showing. His mouth moved wordlessly as he tried to fight off Vex and Qyesar who were holding him firmly down.

The man turned to Qyesar. 'You are his guardian?'

'No, but he was left temporarily in my care.'

'That is close enough. Now, has he Seen before?' At Qyesar's blank look, he added, 'Into time, usually the future.'

'Yes. Only once as far as I know. If there are others, they have not been recorded.'

'Very well. Release him; there is nothing we can do. This boy must now choose his own way.'

Keeping within easy reach, they let him go. Lee instantly stopped fighting and sat up slowly before moving off the table to his feet. He walked, unseeing, down one of the aisles towards the central platform. The Clan Leaders all turned in unison to look at him as he stepped up.

Vex and Qyesar followed him, the Vertex stopping Qyesar at the edge of the platform, waiting. The other man nodded to the Leaders.

'I advise you to send the three-toned Call. This appears to be for us all and it seems urgent. He has suppressed it this long, which is hard for one of the Vanished in an active state.'

The Leaders nodded to him and divided into three groups, ignoring the boy for the time-being. Each group lifted their faces to the ceiling and sent out single, continuous note. The three notes came together in strange harmony, Darkness ringing in the air. Almost instantly, seats were filled with a flurry of Shadow, the walls lined. Each Leader turned to their Clans, examining them carefully. Each nodded, satisfied. All except one. He frowned and re-examined a couple of times further before calling to his Clan.

'Two empty seats. Can they be explained?'

The Clan murmured amongst themselves, working out who was missing.

After a few moments, one man stood and spoke. 'Xophîn and his son, Vlökir. None can account for them.'

The Leader frowned more and turned to Qyesar.

Darkness

'Can the boy wait?'

Lee chose to answer, his voice distant. 'I can hold back for some time if I enter stasis. You have three days.' He sat, his skin greying, cold and hard to the touch.

'Stone...' the Leader murmured before conferring with the others.

In unison, they each faced their Clans. 'As individuals, we cannot hope to find our own within three days. As a people, there is a chance. Find them both. Groups no smaller than three.'

The Vertex divided and the hall emptied. Qyesar sat at the edge of the platform, always watching Lee. 'I was supposed to look after him,' he whispered.

'And you have. When the Vanished See, there is nothing that can be done.'

* * * * * * * * * * * *

Xophîn held Vlökir's hand tight, pulling him through Vantrörkî.

'Two Gatherings so close together. This is not a good sign. Come on, we must hurry.'

Together they ran, through and around Shadow, before Xophîn suddenly stopped. He sensed instability in the area. He turned, watching a broken piece of Shadow, worry lining his face and his grip tightening.

'Father … why has it not moved to the Wasteland?' Vlökir asked.

'It can't. Otherwise it would have. This area has been sealed. It is the way Vantrörkî protects itself from shatters.'

'Shatters?'

'You are too young to have learned of them. Parts of the realm run along faults. From time to time, the Shadow surrounding those faults breaks down. A shatter. Everything in the surrounding area is sealed to contain it, stop it from spreading. Normally there is more warning and any Vertex can leave the area.'

He straightened and looked at his son. 'Do not travel by Shadow. It is too dangerous here. We have to run.' He began to move, Vlökir still processing the information. 'Come on! Run!'

Pushing his son on ahead, Xophîn ran, genuine fear surging through him. Vantrörkî was running out of time. Shatters were becoming more common now.

'We have to get out of here. Keep running, Vlökir. We'll take the long way to the Gathering.' *And the shortest way out of here,* he thought to himself.

Darkness

* * * * * * * * * * * *

A group appeared once more in the hall, addressing the Leaders quickly.

'We have found them, alive but in danger. As they were travelling here, the area they were in sealed off. A shatter. We presume there was no warning, else they would have left. There are two other groups waiting outside for it to reopen. We cannot search until then.'

'There are commands to open the walls to rescue those in a shatter. Open it immediately.'

'The walls do not respond.'

There were a few moments of concerned talk among the Leaders before any spoke again.

'Very well. We will recall the others. Your groups are to remain there and help them as soon as you can.'

The group nodded and vanished as quickly as they had come, the Leaders sending the Call out again. All around, seats filled again.

* * * * * * * * * * * *

Vlökir looked back, only to be pushed on again by his father.

'Don't look behind us. Concentrate on where you're going, on getting out. Don't worry about what's back there. Leave that to me.'

The boy nodded, trying to keep the pace up. A loud creaking could be heard from behind them, like the walls were bending. As it became a thundering rumble, Xophîn pulled his son to the ground, shielding the boy with his body as Shadow fell around them, eventually covering them. The man bit back cries of pain, the shards pressing in on him, tearing at his body. Vlökir, however, could not bear the pain, and screamed as the darkness grew.

* * * * * * * * * * *

Zech continually tested the wall, ready to rush in as soon as soon as it opened. The ten of them could hear the screams, feeling useless.

Suddenly, Zech fell through and stopped, just staring at the destruction before them.

'Quickly. This will soon go to the Wasteland now that the area is open again,' Vituella muttered.

'Understood Captain Lacroixa,' the others replied, panning out as they searched methodically.

They called out both names, hearing no replies. They

moved the broken Shadow aside, but saw neither of them. They continued in this manner until Zech silenced them.

'What is it?' one of the women asked softly.

He hushed her, moving silently through the rubble before dropping to the ground, suddenly digging. 'Help me!' he shouted, the others rushing forwards to help.

After uncovering the pair, they rolled Xophîn over, checking his vitals. Despite the fact he was alive, they could not rouse him.

'At least he's alive,' Zech muttered, pulling the man onto his shoulders.

Vituella lifted the boy to his feet, smiling at him as she sat him up, embracing him gently.

'You're okay now. Can you walk?' she asked, glancing at his injuries. 'You can lean on me.'

Vlökir nodded and began to walk with her, leaning heavily.

Zech glanced upwards. 'We were waiting for a day and searching for half. And now we must walk,' he muttered. 'We may just make it back. 'Airîn, take your group back the fast way. Let them know that we will need medics ready the instant we arrive. Say nothing as to why; that is for Captain Lacroixa to say.'

Airîn nodded and his group vanished. Vlökir closed

his eyes, readying himself to move again.

Vituella frowned and turned to one of the women.

'Take him back. He is small enough for you to carry. We will be able to move faster without him.'

'Yes, Captain,' the woman replied, coaxing the boy away before disappearing.

Vituella turned to Zech. 'Can you run with him?'

'I can. Easily for a few days.'

'Then we run.'

* * * * * * * * * * * *

It was taking all of Qyesar's self-will not to run to Lee and try to shake him awake. Instead, he sat at the edge of the platform, his eyes on the boy. He felt guilty. He had let Maytra down, let Lee down.

Vex walked over to him and sat next to him. 'He'll be fine,' he said, smiling. 'He's meant to do this. He was meant to come here. Everything here, he subconsciously made happen.'

Qyesar looked up. 'No. It's my fault. I let him come and now he's like this.'

'No. You did what felt right to you.'

'Would this have happened had he stayed at the

Darkness

camp?'

To that, Vex had no answer and a moment passed in silence.

'I think he would have found his way here regardless,' he murmured.

A new prophecy.
Already I see it.
That race.
They were always so arrogant.

Now they are gone.
Yet this one remains.
The boy.
Everything is about the boy.

I understand now.

Chapter 12

Questions

There was a knock at the door and it opened slowly. Francin peered nervously around the door. As it opened further, Lyana saw the two women standing behind him.

Smiling, she stood and gestured for them to enter sit down. 'Maytra, it is good to see you again. I trust you are keeping well. And you must be Drásda Mîchka,' she said, turning to the other woman. 'It is a pleasure to finally meet you.'

'And you. I am afraid we cannot stay long, however,' Drásda said quietly. 'We are urgently needed elsewhere. We came for my nephew.'

Francin blanched and turned away, coughing suddenly, as he tended to when nervous.

Maytra caught on instantly. 'Where is he, Francin? Where is Lee?' she asked hurriedly, her tone near deadly, her worry apparent.

The man shifted nervously, passing his weight gently from one foot to the other. 'Lee. Well ... erm ... he's...' he began, trying to find the right words. He was, however, spared from answering when Lyana cut in.

'He's with Qyesar, as was arranged,' she said softly, walking from her desk to the group.

Maytra barely concealed her relief. It was not the case that she did not trust them to look after her son, but that she did not trust her son to remain safe.

'For a moment there, I thought... Well, where are they then?'

'Not in this camp.'

'Then where? What's happened to them?' Maytra asked quickly, her fear for her son rising again.

'Do not worry so. Your son is more than capable of looking after himself, and Qyesar is keeping a close eye on him. They are on Vantrörkî. Qyesar was summoned to learn their ways. Scarien named him as his successor as Ambassador for the Vertex. Hopefully, he will be successful.'

'But why is Lee there then?'

'Your son is curious, loyal and far from stupid. He followed Qyesar as he went to meet his escort. He asked to go with them. Besides, he could not be sent back alone. It

Darkness

was dark, and the lands surrounding this place can be treacherous when you do not know them well. Also, they may have killed him had he not gone. He was not invited, and the Vertex take spying very seriously.'

Maytra sank into a chair, her face pale. All she had heard of the Vertex was dark and dangerous, and she could not help but worry.

Drásda shook her head. 'At least he is safe, Cousin. The Vertex are true to their word and would never normally kill a Cloran.'

'Normally?' Maytra choked.

'Most would never. There is a small issue of those infused with the Deathscent. But the others will keep him safe.'

Maytra frowned, wondering if her cousin could ever be more tactful, but doubting it.

'We cannot wait for him, Maytra. Come, we must go. Others are relying on us.'

'He's just a child…' Maytra whispered.

Drásda smiled. 'He was, but he is growing up fast. Let him. He is a Cloran. He must learn to fly alone.' She touched Maytra's shoulder gently. 'You will see him again.'

Looking at Lyana, the Cloran nodded. 'I am sorry to have intruded on your time. We must be on our way now.'

The camp leader smiled. 'I understand. If you are ever in need of assistance, you know where to turn. The Letrans will support you.'

Drásda pulled Maytra to her feet. 'Come on. Right now, lives are depending on us.'

Lyana stepped back to give them some room. With one sweeping stroke of her hand, Drásda ripped into the Void. The pair nodded one last farewell before stepping through the Tear, which sealed itself up again behind him, a white light moving up it and leaving no trace.

Lyana sighed and walked back to her desk. Leaning heavily on it, she closed her eyes. Was there any control left in her hands? Too much was happening and events were unfolding of their own accord. She could keep the camp running, but everyone was getting distracted. The Elementalists in the camp were particularly restless.

She turned, seeing a bird at the window. She frowned further, walking towards it. She saw the red band around its leg. A messenger hawk of the fourth realm. She let it in, noting the tell-tale silver collar that marked it for Travelling.

She relieved the creature of its message and set out a dish of water and some food for it. It flapped gently onto the desk, weary after its long flight. Unlike when people used the Gates, it was found that birds had to travel the entire distance through a small tunnel in the Void. How they knew how to leave was still unknown, but they made very reliable messengers.

Taking her eyes off the bird, she unfurled the slip of paper. She looked at it, frowning at the dot-dash patterns. Sighing, she sat down and began to translate.

> To: Scarien Éscaronôvic
> From: James Greenwood
> Subject: RE: Gathering
>
> I understand what you are trying to say, but we still believe it possible that the Zyrons will try and stage their next fight here. This realm is already in turmoil. We are currently at war. From what we have heard of your realm, we are worried it could lead to collapse.
>
> We are ready to intervene should signs of collapse appear. We are not overly worried. In the last century there were two, much larger wars. It is in our nature to battle. Nation is constantly pitted against nation.
>
> I warn you again. The science and

technology could potentially all be adapted to your realms of magick. Some of what we have is dangerous, deadly. We cannot gather together. We need all our separate factions to monitor Gate activity. The chance that someone may come for our weapons must be prevented.

The proposal of a Gather to brief everyone is also unrealistic. As you know, our realm is much larger than any of yours. Some of our countries are bigger than your realms.

As a Human, I may know little of your ways and politics, but I know ours. As a tactical advisor, I recommend you reconsider. To pull your people away from here to sort troubles elsewhere will leave this realm more vulnerable.

Lyana shook her head. She mulled over the message, wondering what had been said before it. Judging from its state, it had been delayed for whatever reason.

She looked at the date. 29th Aug. She wondered what the man meant by Aug. It took her a few minutes to make the connection to August. *You're getting out of practice, girl. How can you expect to lead when you forget things like that?* Crossing the room, she sent a summons to the Inter-Realm

Connections Advisor: Kerianna Mrya.

As she waited, she read over it again. What was Scarien saying? She did not know much about Earth, but she knew it was big. Very big. Catré was considered overly large and yet it was only a third of its size. And the population was phenomenal. Over six billion residents. Plus a much more abundant wildlife. And they were destroying their beautiful world. She could never understand that. Why would they?

This James Greenwood was correct to say that a Gathering on Earth was unfeasible. Separate briefings would have to be conducted. Also, it was so rich in inventions that were constantly being improved. It was a known target of the Zyrons, so why would Greenwood have to clarify the risk to Scarien. He knew the dangers.

Everything about the message seemed wrong somehow. Fake. If only she knew why.

A tall brunette walked into the office while she was reading it again. 'You called ma'am?'

'Lyana,' Lyana automatically corrected, 'and yes. I did call. Please could you take a look at this?'

Kerianna took the message and studied it for a few minutes before handing it back. 'What is it you want to know?'

'Firstly, what does the date correspond to? Secondly, what do you make of it? Something doesn't feel right to me.'

Kerianna sat down and thought for a few moments. 'The date could be only three weeks ago. August twenty-ninth corresponded to Kirter first. But judging by the paper, it's from the August before, or Triannon seventh.'

'That would make it eight months old.'

'Yes. Also, I am wondering about this James Greenwood. There is no one by that name that I am aware of. Our liaison is Jay Fenwood. The only way to know if this really came from him is to send people to them and maintain constant, direct contact.

'The other issue is the message itself. Scarien wanted to keep the Elementalists on Earth. The people there are under constant threat and the Zyrons certainly have the realm in their sights. The few Letrans we have placed there are barely enough to monitor the realm. There are some gifted natives who have joined together to help.'

Kerianna carefully tore off the corner of the message and burnt it in her hand, lighting it with a small spark from her finger. Bright purple flames shot up, licking the ceiling, the smoke produced tasting bitter in their mouths. Kerianna's forehead sweated as she fought to bring the flames down and under control.

'What was that?' Lyana asked.

'A problem. This paper is not from the fourth realm. It will take more tests to determine who sent it, but Scarien always burnt his letters. Had the whole parchment gone up, I doubt even he would have been able to stop it. The smoke is a dampener, preventing our skills from working.'

They both turned to the hawk on the table, which had begun to stare intently at them.

~*That bird is no messenger hawk,*~ Kerianna said silently, blocking her thoughts from the creature.

Lyana looked at her. She herself had never been able to communicate telepathically, despite her race.

~*Go back to the door. I'll contain it. I doubt it is a bird at all. It is possibly an Aviana from Simpru. They are a sub-race of that realm. The Prunœns have been trying to keep their numbers under control, but they are very hard to find.*~

Lyana walked casually to the door, grabbing some papers on her way. 'You see what you can find. I need to pass these on to Daesir.'

Kerianna nodded. As soon as Lyana was by the door, she turned, a fiery cage appearing around the bird, binding it. Its form rippled into that of a dwarf-like creature. It tried to unleash its own magickal attack, but could not get past the barrier.

Lyana watched in amazement. 'Now what?'

'Well, I believe it would be best to inform the Prunœns and see what they wish to do with it.'

Lyana nodded. 'I still think we should send some people to Earth. Do we have anyone acquainted with their customs?'

'I can make a list for you, Lyana. And I'll move this thing to a more permanent home.'

'Thank you, Kerianna. Could you inform the Prunœns as well? They need to know that one of these creatures is loose among the realms. They may know their intentions.'

'Of course.' She nodded politely before leaving the room, the cage floating on before her.

Once the door swung shut, Lyana lowered her face to her palms, sighing. *What would Scarien do?* she asked herself. *What would Mattias do?*

The temporary leader of the Letrans closed her eyes, drifting into a thoughtful sleep, her head in her arms. But as she did, all she could see was the shooting purple fire. *Mattias chose wrong. I'm no leader,* was her last thought before sleep took her.

I can feel it.
With every breath the boy draws.
I am growing stronger.

The Balance is shifting.
He cannot fight it.
This is my chance.

But what else…?

Chapter 13

Dragons

Verton landed amongst the Earth Dragons. Their healing touch was needed on Cyphia and it would be quicker to stop for the fold and then continue, rather than take the boy back and then return for them.

~*His injury runs deep. Deeper than we can heal. While he should last the journey home, he may not survive much longer,*~ he called to them.

~*The Pillar would not have called if it was his time so soon. He has to survive. If this were his injury, we would tend it now,*~ the largest of the flock replied. He turned to the others, addressing them loudly. ~*Call the Flames. We need them to heal the true injury. This is but a shadow,*~ he instructed.

Several of the smaller Dragons took flight, leaving the plains for the fire fields in the south, able to fly faster than some of their larger siblings.

A general sense of readiness surged through the group, and the flock took to the skies as one. Each pair of wings rose and fell out of sync, the smallest beating her wings twice for every stroke the largest took.

The great brown lead the group and they never broke formation. Verton was always near centre, Camer held gently but securely in his claws. Here, the boy was safe from any surprise attacks from other Dragons. This realm was one at war. Temporary truces and the Dance were the only peace they had now.

After a short while in the air, a flurry of oranges, reds and more golds joined them. The usual animosity between Dragon types was unheeded then as they took their place among the flock. This was a time to work together, as was their Dance of Life every year on their realm. This translated roughly to a century upon the fourth realm.

~*We thank you for alerting us. We felt a disturbance in the flames, yet could not place it,*~ one of the deep red Dragons said across the flock.

~*We were obliged to. Fire and Earth have a close connection. Both will suffer if we cannot work together. In times of torment, we can be allies.*~

~*Truer words were never spoken. If only we could change our nature. We may be allies today, but it does not change our stand upon return. Let us fly.*~

Together the large group picked up speed quickly and made their way back to Cyphia. Back to a child in need of their help.

* * * * * * * * * * * *

Mattias frowned, deep in a magickally-induced sleep. His dreams were strange, full of meaning, but hard to make sense of.

Magnificent beasts filled the air. So many colours, so many sizes. Their wings were wide, each powerful beat keeping them aloft. Some of the smaller ones would glide often, their lighter bodies more readily held by the wind. Dragons. They could be nothing else. Their flight was graceful as they sped around in the sky.

A flaming-red let loose a jet of flame up into the air, the other fiery colours mirroring the action. The other colours, however, had no input; only the oranges, reds and golds seemed to have the capability. The rest flew around them in perfect harmony as if this were a dance.

~*Dragons of Fire,*~ he thought abstractly. The moment he spoke it to himself, the thought was lost to the dream.

His gaze turned to the surrounding landscape. A great lake covered much of the land to the west, gushing rivers filling it from snow-topped mountains of deep blue. Here was the home of the Dragons of Water.

To the east a vast mist of swirling colour filled the air. Very little could be seen of the ground, the focus being drawn entirely to the skies.

To the south, great volcanoes and fire holes spurted irregularly, seeming to fill the sky with liquid fire. Just looking at the area made Mattias feel hot, burning.

Finally, in the north were great plains with long rolling hills surrounding them. The grass was the greenest he had ever seen and the land seemed perfectly kept, not wild.

The divisions between each land were startlingly distinct. It was apparent which Dragons occupied each area, the boundaries set out for all to see.

The Dragons around him flew together in a central area, not bound by the four elements. There was only a vast nothingness intermingling with a pillar of white light which shot up out of the nothing into the heavens, rippling like a flowing river. Thin, hair-like strands waved around, attached to the pillar and vanishing into rippling air.

~*Off into other realms...*~

Similar waving strands returned from the ripples, but were black, sinking into the void.

~*Life and death. Now how do I know that?*~

Darkness

His gaze turned upwards as he suddenly found himself below the flock. ~*This was long ago. A time of peace. There is no peace now.*~ Briefly, he wondered how he could know that, but the thought dissipated and he was content to watch.

The fire that had been released swirled around the pillar, weaving around it and forming an intricate pattern. Finishing their breath, the Fire Dragons dived down before returning to the dance. The boy could feel the heat once more, surging through him.

Almost instantly, that heat was soothed as the Dragons of Water, coloured with blues, cyans and silvers, circled out around the flock, flying directly upwards. Streams of ice escaped them, shooting up to the centre of the dance, where they collided. Great flakes of snow rained down upon them, yet they looked warmer than true snow. The fire spiralling around merged with each flake, forming something indistinct.

Those clad in almost clear scales with hints of yellows purples and silver dropped low below the group, even lower than Mattias. Their mouths opened wide and he could almost see the air vibrating up around him. The falling flakes began to swell, becoming lighter, floating in the air. Their surface seemed to ripple with a breeze as more air was pumped into them

The remaining Dragons, the greens, golds and browns, breathed lightly over them and they formed a stone-hard coating, spinning gracefully in the air.

The strange creations fell towards the void and stopped suddenly, floating at the border of nothing and everything. The air around them took different sheens, mirroring the colours of the Dragons around. Now he could see. They were eggs, and would eventually hatch. The glow below him was soft and gentle, like a dream.

He watched as the colours clustered themselves to align with the element they belonged to. He knew he had just witnessed the most amazing events. His mind longed to see it again someday, for real.

~*But this is a dream,*~ he suddenly thought as he marvelled at the beauty.

Whether it was him thinking that, or for some other reason, Mattias felt himself being pulled back, the images swimming and fading as he tried to cling onto them. After only a few moments, only the memory of the experience remained.

* * * * * * * * * * * *

Darkness

Camer and Mattias lay in the infirmary, both beds close together. The Dragons had taken a humanoid form resembling the elven race that has permeated mythology. They were tall, graceful and fair-skinned, their ears long and pointed at the tip. Their hair and eyes were the only indication of their element, being the exact colour their scales had been. They were clad in a strange, flowing cloth which rippled in an unknown wind, sometimes almost resembling their wings. They all crowded around the pair, preparing their own magick, their eyes glowing faintly as their energy grew.

The Dragons of Fire joined hands, and closed their eyes, the healing glow warm and bright. The wound seemed to take forever to even begin to heal, the poison running deep and resisting extraction. However, it did start to close, and once it reached the same stage that Camer's was at, the Earth Dragons could begin.

Pausing the flow, they all prepared to begin again, simultaneously. Both wounds had to close at the same rate for the process to be successful. The overspill of healing magick affected all in the palace, giving them new strength and vigour. Even Qyan, still drained as he was, felt its effects as he tossed in bed.

They were done fairly quickly with both elements

working together. They assured themselves that there would be no further problems, checking both wounds carefully. However, the pair would forever bear matching pale scars running down the lengths of their arms. Even the strongest magick could never remove that.

And so, their task complete, the Dragons withdrew. They walked together a while out into the hills. There they shifted, their garments unfurling into their astonishing wings, their bodies then growing, scales forming and hair vanishing. Once fully reptilian, they took flight, as one flock for home. They would go their separate ways once in their own realm.

* * * * * * * * * * * *

The boys woke together with a start. They looked at each other and began to laugh in strange relief, the magick still strong, lifting their spirits. They had both made it through their ordeal and were feeling on top of the world.

The girls, having sensed their waking left their beds to see them. They darted into the room only a few minutes later, diving onto the boys. Hugging each other in turn, the laughter lessened for a moment or so, but did not disappear altogether.

Darkness

~*What's so funny?*~ Scortia asked, confused.

Her expression only heightened the boys' laughter, which very quickly became infectious. The healing magick of the Dragons had not just healed their physical wound and given them new strength, it had healed the worst part of their grief. They could all finally concentrate on what needed to be done without dwelling greatly on the past. Scortia and Caya, finding themselves in similar hysterics, had no idea why they were laughing, and neither did Camer or Mattias. All they knew was that a huge weight had been lifted and they felt able to laugh for the first time since Scarien's demise.

Gradually, it abated, leaving them breathless. Camer examined the scar on his arm, still grinning. He stifled further laughter as he turned to Mattias.

~*It's always you who causes trouble. And it's always your trouble that takes us both close to death.*~

Mattias faked a scowl playfully. ~*You're the one who gets involved uninvited. You could turn the other way. At least we match now.*~

Both boys stuck their tongues out at each other, the brush with death breaking the tension as only it could.

Scortia smiled. 'It seems strange-'

Everyone cringed as her voice broke the easy silence of the room. They had become so used to the intimacy of telepathy among themselves that her words sounded distant and unfeeling, not to mention creating unnecessary sound.

She laughed lightly. 'That's just what I mean. It wasn't that long ago that we all spoke like this – well, I am presuming that you two did as well – and found telepathy strange when we learnt of it. Now, while it's fine to laugh or cry, we barely speak. Only when there are others around who we don't know well enough do we use our voices.'

Caya looked suddenly pensive. *~If I remember right, I used to hate talking without talking,~* she said softly, she and Scortia sharing an inward smile at her phrase. *~It freaked me out to no end. Now, however...~* She trailed off, not needing to finish her sentence.

Mattias and Camer looked at each other, knowing exactly what the other two meant. It was only a couple of months before that they had discovered their telepathy.

Caya shrugged. *~It's more convenient, anyway, to talk like this. It's quicker and private. Most people can't hear what we're saying, although there are ways to eavesdrop.~*

~Also, we can talk across greater distances and even between realms and dimensions if we have to,~ Scortia added.

Mattias smiled. *~Whenever we want, wherever we want. And the best part is being able to pick up more readily on emotion. It's harder to deceive someone you know through*

Darkness

thought-speak.~

~Is that an advantage though?~ Caya asked playfully.

They thought about it in silence for a while before Mattias turned to Camer, something having been on his mind since they had awoken.

~There is something different about you,~ he commented, his statement also a question as to what had occurred while he had been unconscious.

Camer shrugged lightly. *~I am still myself,~* he said plainly. *~You will understand when it is your time.~* He understood now the secrecy of the Dragons and did not wish to be the one to divulge their secrets.

Mattias shook his head in slight annoyance, but knew better than to probe further. Camer would not reveal anything about the events until he was ready, or, more likely until they had each experienced it themselves. He was very good at keeping his silence when he chose to.

Scortia tactfully followed her brother's lead, thinking of something to change the conversation to. The conversation, however, stayed on track, thanks to Caya.

Caya was not as understanding as the other two. She frowned at the pair and poked Camer rather hard, her inquisitive mind needing answers, and her love for Dragons fuelling that need. *~Come on. The Dragons must have shown you something cool.~* When he shook his head, she continued. ~*Why did they call you the Guardian of Earth?*~

Camer closed his eyes, his transformation even more apparent as he inhaled slowly. He seemed more sturdy, more authoritative than he had before. As he exhaled, he spoke calmly. ~*As the Dragon said: 'The others will be shown when it is their time.' So be patient, Caya. Be patient and you, yourself, will see.*~ He paused, opening his eyes. They sparkled strangely, green flickering across the mud-brown of his irises. ~*Although,*~ he continued, sounding almost like himself again, ~*you will be the last to find out, Guardian of Water. As the youngest of the elements, Water must wait till all others have seen before she is permitted to do so.*~

Caya's mouth dropped open, and they all saw the signs of angry comments to come. Mattias quickly changed the topic to the vivid memory of his dream, averting her coming retort. ~*I had the strangest dream earlier. About the Dragons. I'm not even sure if it was even a dream...*~

Caya fell silent and turned her attention to Mattias, intrigued as soon as she heard the word 'Dragons'. She sat on Camer's bed, staring intently at him.

Scortia looked at her twin. She had always been the more impulsive of the pair, despite her own disappearance up the mountain. However, she had believed her twin's personality to have improved somewhat over the past few months, ever since she had discovered her talents with Water. But when she got an idea, that sense of improvement had vanished altogether.

For a long time, Mattias was silent, thinking over what he remembered and wondering how to relay it to the others. He mused over the unusual vividness of the memory. As the trio of listeners became more impatient, he finally began to speak, revealing to them what it was he had seen, with all the detail he could remember. All the while, he longed to be there, in that realm, to experience it fully, rather than just through sight.

The Dance.
Such beauty.
But I may never Dance again.

With my queen by my side.
She must not waken.
The Balance will be restored.

She will stop me.

Chapter 14

Prophecy

Vlökir remained in the arms of Sarýya, watching the walls. His eyes showed his fear for his father and he desperately hoped that he would be okay. A full day had passed since Sarýya had brought him back to the Gathering. He knew it would take time for the team to get his father back, but he was getting anxious.

He turned his gaze to the stranger, Qyesar. The man had not moved from his position, still sitting with his eyes on the stone boy. From the mumblings around him, Vlökir had discovered that the boy was not really stone, but one of the Vanished who had used Gargoyle to keep a recent vision from spilling out, for it was one he had to show, rather than tell.

Qyesar sighed, reaching out to the boy with his thoughts. He was not, himself, telepathic, but knew Lee could probably sense his thoughts. He wanted to reassure and comfort the boy. But he could not. Sitting and waiting was all he could do.

He had not a clue as to how long he had spent in Vantrörkî. Time just melted by and had very little meaning to the shadows. All he knew was that they had been there too long. He should never have let Lee come.

No, they would have killed him had I not. Someone more reliable than Francin should have been keeping an eye on him. What will I tell his mother?

Vex returned to Qyesar's side, crouching next to him.

'Come, we have some food. We may not eat ourselves, but your body needs sustaining. More than two days have passed since you had any nourishment. Maybe longer, I do not know.' He smiled, the sight strangely disturbing. 'I doubt the boy will be happy if we starved you. The Vanished are one race never to anger, for they are stronger than they ever showed.'

Qyesar allowed the Vertex to lead him away from the platform to a table, laden with various foods. He blinked, hardly believing his eyes. The best food imported directly from the fourth realm was right before him, including the all-important bacon.

His stomach rumbled in anticipation. He turned to Vex, his gaze questioning.

'When we liaised with Scarien, it was all he would

eat. He had told us that most of the camp food was imported from the fourth realm, usually as the final product.'

Qyesar nodded. 'The food is cheaper, and tastes better than if we import the animals to grow it on Catré. It's untainted by magick.'

Vex shrugged. 'Instead, it is tainted by chemicals. Nothing is truly pure. Not even there.'

Qyesar shrugged, not caring as he made himself a bacon, egg and sausage sandwich. He was no use to Lee if he was starving. The first bite reminded him of his first introduction to such foods; it tasted heavenly.

His attention, however, was rapidly turned from his meal to a commotion at the edge of the great hall. He watched as a man was carried in, unconscious, on the back of another.

'All Clan members are now present and accounted for,' called the Clan Leaders, the Vertex flitting quickly into their seats once more, two remaining with the unconscious man.

Qyesar watched as a boy broke free of another, running to the man. Vlökir silently asked to help the men tending to his father.

The Leaders waited for the commotion to die down

and took up their positions on the platform. Still standing, they waited a few moments more.

The two Repairers nodded to their Leaders, guiding Vlökir silently through the process to help his father. The boy had natural talent, and once they could get started, the Gathering could proceed without further interruption.

'Seer awaken. Reveal to us your truth. Show us the future that you have deemed to be for all our eyes,' the Leaders said with one voice.

The stone statue that was Lee cracked, the sound deafening in the sudden silence. Slowly, the crack spread along the surface of the stone, more fractures splintering off from it. A white light shone brightly from within, only to be absorbed by the shadows around.

Qyesar started forwards, dropping his sandwich. However, Vex lifted a hand to stop him, shaking his head slightly. After a frustrated look at the Vertex, Qyesar turned his gaze back to Lee, sinking into a seat.

A strange hissing voice echoed around the room. 'The time is coming. He will soon be among us.'

The light grew, a shape forming above their heads. A great Dragon appeared to be flying, its wings rising and forming regularly. However, the background to the scene had not yet materialised.

Darkness

The scene came into view slowly, in patches. The sky through which the Dragon flew was bright and clear. Qyesar marvelled at the sight. He had only heard tales of Dragons, and like most, had never even dreamed that he would really see one, even if it was only through a vision. Also, the images were so vivid, it was as though he were really there, the hall they were in slowly fading, giving way to something more spectacular.

A ground began to appear below them, seemingly several feet of air separating them from the construct. Despite the feeling of the chair beneath him, Qyesar could not help but feel as though he were floating. He would much rather see what was supporting him.

Other Dragons came into sight, Dragons of all colours, meeting together at the heart of their realm. Here was the crux of all existence: the point of life and death.

At this point was an everlastingly tall white pillar, laced with silver. Upon closer observation, other colours could be seen, rippling with such rapidity, that the white appeared unbroken. This pillar was set in an everlasting pit of darkness. Nothing was there, not even air. Nothing could exist. No light, no shadow.

As Qyesar lifted his gaze back to the Dragons, he saw that, at random points along the pillar, tendrils thinner than the threads of a spider web emerged, laced with varying colours. More and more colours were developing as time passed.

Similar tendrils came from the pit, but were as black as the Nothing they came from, or went to. The threads appeared to move slightly, but only under very close observation. Miniscule beads of light travelled along the threads from the pillar, while beads of darkness moved along the black threads towards the pit.

A cycle? Qyesar pondered. *But of what?*

The Dragons captured his attention once more as they mingled in the air. They appeared to be communicating, their words lost by the nature of the vision. It did not seem like these were peaceful creature, but instead, it felt like this were a temporary truce in a raging battle.

Their flight weaved around the pillar, rarely passing through a thread. When a Dragon passed through a thread, it would vanish, and one of the dark threads would vanish also, as if they had been severed. Part of Qyesar realised that a creature or plant had died at that point. Yet these occurrences did not seem to be mistakes. The threads to be cut would move into the flight path of a Dragon.

The random movements the Dragons made gave the

Darkness

illusion of a dance. The dance produced a strange melody, as if the movement alone could make music. The sound echoed clearly through the hall, beautiful in nature. Though the Dragons made no sounds themselves, their dance was harmonious, gaining complexity and depth as the motions changed.

Before long, it was nearly impossible to discern the elements of each Dragon. The colours would merge, forming new hues. There was no longer a separation of Earth, Air, Fire or Water. They were all one.

Suddenly, the Dragons of Fire broke free from the group, streams of liquid fire escaping them and snaking around and into the great pillar. The pillar took on the fiery appearance, flames spiralling out only to curl back in.

As the Dragons rejoined the group, the dance became more rapid, hotter. The heat surrounded them, almost unbearable and Qyesar felt it prickling up his body, even though the hall was actually quite cold.

A wave of blue and turquoise rippled through the flames as the Water Dragons descended to the base of the pillar. The water cascaded up the pillar like a waterfall in reverse. Combining with the flames, great, hot snowflakes were formed, held in place by the pillar, prevented from falling. The heat lessened also, becoming less intense and much more bearable.

The Dragons of Air took their turn, circling above the group with such speed, it seemed they were just a ring of colour. The wind they generated rippled around them, enveloping the flakes and pulling them free of the pillar so that they were suspended in the air. The pillar was once again white, the orbs around growing slightly in size, the essences of Fire, Water and Air swirling within.

Finally, as the dance became lighter, the Dragons of Earth flew upwards, towards the orbs. Each breathed lightly over a cluster, their shells of stone forming. The pillar shot out threads to each of these constructs, the pit doing the same to complete the circle. However, while the beads of light moved away from the pillar, the beads of darkness also moved towards the spheres, rather than away from them.

As the orbs clustered together, glowing light surrounded them. Their groups were unequal, but there were no more than seven in each cluster. The glowing eggs sank down towards the ground. The tendrils retreated, their work complete.

It was during this process that a loud sound echoed around, as if something had suddenly snapped. As the scene rotated, it became obvious what had happened. A great crack had appeared in the pillar. The Dragons recoiled, their dance ending prematurely. The eggs, no longer suspended by the melody, began to free fall towards the ground.

After only the briefest of hesitations, the Dragons swooped down to rescue their eggs. The shells would not be strong enough to survive any impact until they had taken on their final colours.

Together, using the elements and their own bodies, they managed to guide every egg safely to their resting point, floating on the line that separated dark and light. A wave of apprehension and fear swept through the group and Qyesar found himself leaning forward, strangely on edge. What would this mean for the eggs? The Dragons could not afford to lose even one, let alone a whole batch.

Deciding swiftly amongst themselves, the Dragons turned and flew to their respective homes, letting nature takes its course. If the eggs were to survive, they would. Everything happened for a reason greater than even they could fathom.

The scene saw the Dragons becoming smaller specks in the sky before suddenly changing, now focussing on the eggs around the pillar. The grey stone protecting them was hardening, taking on the colour of the glow that surrounded them. These colours determined which Dragon would hatch. The vision slowly moved closer, gradually isolating a single cluster. It very quickly became clear that one of the eggs was different. There was no glow about it and the stone did not take on an elemental colour. Instead, the grey darkened, slowly becoming the blackest of blacks.

The scene faded and the Vertex murmured uncertainly, clearly disturbed by what was to come. But the vision was not finished, and the blackness around them only became apparent as a voice could be heard.

'The Balance is tipping. This is his time. Only her birth can restore order to the realms,' hissed the voice they had heard earlier.

'She will not come. It is up to them now,' a more melodic voice whispered.

'They will fail.' The word fail echoed away slowly.

Snapshot scenes appeared, one after another. They lingered for barely a second, just long enough to see.

Mount Zircon, the sky blood red. The blackest of clouds rumbling around it. People were fighting, the sounds of battle deafening. Qyetari filled the air.

The fly-like Haveen retreating to their underground homes, their world crumbling around them. Pieces of the sky fell upon them.

Darkness

The great storms of Earth, devastating lives. With nowhere to run, people died where they stood. Civilisations were ripped apart.

The great hive of the Dracona crumbling. The Finders were shattered, the Gemstone trying to protect her people. The colours faded as stone fell apart.

So many realms, so many races. Some were known, others were not. Everywhere showed the destruction that was to come. There would be nowhere to run, nowhere to hide.

The images faded before being replaced by a scene of red. This again faded slowly. The same red appeared, but there was a cliff edge visible below it. They were looking at a blood-red sky. The scene faded again and a great cracking sound echoed around them, followed by slow splintering.

A girl's voice rang out over the noise. 'Help me hold it!'

The scene materialised, patchy at times and riddled with noise. A great black crack had appeared in the sky, smaller cracks breaking out, growing from the central one.

Several figures were standing on the cliff, a girl with light brown hair right against the edge. She was too far away for Qyesar to make out her face. There was a symbol glowing on her forehead as a white energy shot from her hands towards the crack. She seemed to be trying to pull it shut again, shouting at the others to help.

One of those further back shouted to her, 'It's too much for you to hold! Even with all four of you. You're not ready! You'll get sucked in. Leave it!'

The others were also shouting, their words lost in the growing noise. Three were further forward than the rest, two of them holding the other back.

The scene went black very suddenly, silence falling. From the darkness of the vision, a pair of golden eyes opened.

The vision ended there, the hall coming back into view. A murmur of unrest spread throughout the Vertex, the vision having unsettled them quite clearly.

Qyesar turned his gaze to Lee. The boy looked older now, at least twenty years of age. A streak of blue weaved through his blond hair. Casually, unfazed by what he had shown them, he stepped down from the platform and walked towards Qyesar. Up close, it was easier to see the transformation.

'It makes sense now. All my dreams, the visions. They all make sense. I know what I must do.' The boy looked up at Qyesar and though his face bore a smile, there was a tear in his eye. His left eye. The eye that had turned golden.

It will be so.
The Fires are burning.
The Waters are churning.
The Earth is crumbling.
The Air will become still.

And from the silence…

Chapter 15

Towards Destiny

~So, Dragons are made, not born? They physically create their young?~ asked Caya disbelievingly. ~Are you sure it wasn't just a dream?~

~I saw that realm first hand. He could not have dreamed such a sight. Not with such accuracy,~ Camer retorted.

Caya screwed up her face. ~But ... that's just wrong.~

~They probably see it as completely natural. Imagine what they must think of us.~ Mattias laughed at the thought. ~It's just different natures.~

Caya wrinkled her nose slightly and Scortia prodded her hard.

~Be more open-minded. You're the one obsessed with the Dragons.~

They all laughed, barely hearing the knock at the door.

Tæmî pushed the door open slowly, peering around it. Her face clearly filled with relief, seeing them all.

'Good. You're awake. I need to speak to you, and it cannot wait any longer.'

Caya opened her mouth to say something, but closed it quickly as the empress strode across the room, muttering a small enchantment.

~*Containment,*~ murmured Scortia. ~*A crude way of preventing intruders and unwanted listeners.*~

~*It's probably the best the Cyphians have. Every race is limited,*~ Mattias replied.

~*Why not just use thought-speak?*~ Scortia asked him, clearly baffled.

~*You can listen in on thought-speak quite easily,*~ Camer said.

~*You can eavesdrop on the conversations, when you know how,*~ Caya said at the same time.

The pair looked at each other and shared a smile. Caya continued what she had been saying.

~*Besides, it may not be a capability of the Cyphians.*~

'No, it is not,' Tæmî said, turning. 'No Cyphian can participate in telepathy, but we all have the capability to hear it when in range.' She looked at Scortia. 'My methods may be crude, but they are effective nonetheless.' She looked at Caya. 'The method of eavesdropping you referred to. I presume you meant when you are detached from your own body.' In response to the girl's nod, she continued. 'All Cyphians are partially detached from their bodies anyway. We do not know why, but it seems to be the cause for our immunity to the shift change.'

Mattias nodded, making a mental note to ask Caya about this technique at a later time. 'So what do you wish to speak to us about?' he asked the empress.

'Scarien was a good friend of mine, even though we lost touch over the last few years. Before he left Cyphia for the last time, he told me that you would come here, years in the future. I never forgot that. It was as though he had seen into the future himself, despite never having that gift.

'Anyway, I was to invite you in immediately and pass on a message to you, for he knew he would not be with you. Then, he asked me to lead you to the Destiny Halls.

'I intended to do all this instantly, but when you first arrived in my domain, I could not come for you. And when you left so suddenly, it was all I could do to send the Dragons' aid. The hostility from your assailant filled the realm.

'When you were returned here, you were injured, in need of rest. And so I delayed further. Now, I can delay no more, for forces are moving in Cyphia, and many are hostile.'

'A message? From my father?' Mattias asked, feeling his anger levels rising. 'Why not send someone to bring us to you earlier. Before the Havern attacked?'

'I could not. You do not understand the workings of this realm. "Empress" is not just a title. It is far more than that. I cannot express my apology enough to you, but my people will always come first.'

An awkward silence followed, Mattias still angry at her, his glare so intense and burning that she seemed to shrink beneath it.

'So what was this message?' Caya asked quietly, breaking the tension.

Tæmî turned to her. 'Scarien, as I said, fully expected himself to not be here with you. He knew what he had to do to get you on your way, and knew it would break his Oath. He was that sort of man. Always working for a greater purpose.

'His first message was for his daughters, as though he knew you would be here at the same time. He asked you to see him as soon as you can, for he may be able to offer you the advice you need, even beyond death. Also, he wishes to see you grown, and hopes you are well.

'His second message was for all of you. His words were: "The shadows of Life are not those of Death. Walk the right shadows to find the answers. When Death awakens, flee the light and restore balance, for Death is born of Life and Life is born of Death. This is a cycle that must never be broken."

'His words made little sense to me, but I presume he had his reasons for being cryptic. He trusted you to find the answers you need.

'He then added that where one finds solace, the other finds danger; be ever vigilant for never are you all safe.'

Mattias frowned and tried to think over it. The words were something Scarien would say, but they made no sense. He understood the last part, and wondered why it needed saying. They knew to be on guard at all times.

Tæmî watched them carefully. 'There is one more thing I must say while you are here. Death rides the wind and will come ever more swiftly if you cannot find the answers.'

Another silence passed among them as the children strove to makes sense of her words. It was far too cryptic and they wondered what relevance it held to their destiny.

Eventually, Camer turned to Tæmî. 'Can you lead us to the Destiny Halls? We could not find a way in.'

'And you never would, for the entrances lie with the Empresses. Only we can open the way forward.' She smiled and turned. 'We do not have much time. Forces are moving in Dra'noxia. Follow me.'

She led them out of the room, checking the hallway carefully. Hurriedly, she made for the nearest staircase, ushering them down before following behind. The stairs took them down beneath the castle, and quite quickly, the lights above them, illuminating the way, faded into darkness.

At this point, Mattias took the lead, holding his hand out ahead, a bright flame shining in his palm. The light clearly showed their surroundings. In the flickering light the walls glistened. They were now deep below the castle and the tunnel walls were damp. Small creatures that the children could not identify covered the edges of the floor, scattering away from their feet and the light. Similar, but larger, creatures covered the ceiling. Scortia clung to Caya, avoiding the bug-like animals as though her life depended upon it. Her fear for any insect-like creatures was shining through, and Caya could not help but stifle a laugh.

Still trying not to laugh at her twin, she cast a were-light above them to give them more light. That way, they could all see more clearly where they were putting their

Darkness

feet. It also gave Scortia some relief as the creatures were a little further away from her thanks to their intolerance of light.

Eventually, the stairs ended, and they found themselves in a narrow, slippery passageway. Tæmî cast a nervous look behind her and ushered the children on.

'We're being followed,' she murmured. 'They are far behind us at the moment, but I can still pick up on their thoughts.'

'I thought you said only an Empress could lead someone this way,' Camer muttered.

'I did. They are following me, so I am involuntarily leading them. We need to find some way to lose them.'

An uneasy feeling passed through the group as they picked up speed, taking care with their footing. The ground was getting wetter and more uneven as they travelled down the dark passage.

The darkness seemed to stretch on for hours and the walk was tiring. With no sense of time, Mattias' watch having stopped, they had no way of knowing how long they had been underground.

A sharp sound behind them made them turn suddenly, the four gathering around Tæmî to protect their guide from whatever was coming. Elements at the ready, they tensed, scanning their surroundings. Their hands seemed to be lost in the centre of glowing orbs, the essences of the elements snaking around them.

Tæmî shuddered, her voice shaking as she whispered, 'I cannot read their thoughts, but I can sense that they are near. It is as though they have no thought … as though they are half-dead.'

A shudder ran up all five spines as a high-pitched squeal pierced the air, like sharp fingernails dragging across stone.

Life from the Void.
Life fills it.

Death from the Shadows.
Death rules them.

That is how it should have been.
What went wrong?

What am I missing?

Chapter 16

Ribbons

Maytra blinked as she emerged from the Tear into the bright realm beyond. A flash of light made her turn to look behind, but the Tear was gone, only a slight shimmer in the air telling of it ever existing. Even as she watched, the shimmer faded to nothing, her view now unbroken.

I'll never get used to this, she thought to herself. Turning back, she saw that Drásda had already sped on ahead. Shaking her head slightly out of annoyance, she hurried after her cousin.

Drásda kept up her pace, not waiting for Maytra to get her bearings. The experienced Jumper had no time to waste. Lives were on the line and speed was of the essence.

'Where are we going?' Maytra asked breathlessly as she finally drew level to her cousin. 'Why have you brought me here? And where is here?'

Drásda continued for a while longer in silence before

finally speaking. 'Things are not always as they seem. We are here to put things right and complete the cycle,' she replied in a level tone.

'But what do you mean by that?'

'Stop asking questions and come with me. You will see soon enough so long as you hurry up.'

Maytra frowned, but did as she was told and fell silent, scanning the realm they were now in. She longed to stop and just admire the beauty around her. She could feel the power of the realm already growing within her. Magick buzzed in the air. The whole realm looked, felt, sounded and smelt wonderful. It was perfect. It felt right.

The vegetation beneath their feet was an intriguing mixture of blues and reds, appearing golden in places, especially in the distance. It resembled very bushy grass and was so springy beneath their feet that Maytra felt like she was floating over the surface of the realm. There were small patches of flowers all over the ground. Their petals were spiky and gleamed with strangely vivid colours. They sparkled magickally and their scent mingled in the light breeze. The smell was indescribable, but filled the concerned woman with a new sense of peace and contentment she had never before felt.

Turning her gaze to the horizon, Maytra blinked at

the spot where sky met land, her pace slowing to take in the spectacular view. Great ribbons of light sprung from random places in the sky, spreading out with all different colours. The ribbons intertwined, some merging to form new colours, creating a beautiful, rippling pattern high above them.

Upon close inspection of the landscape, she could see that it, too, appeared to ripple, but not with the breeze. The moving light of the ribbons was reflected slightly by the ground with all its multitude of colour.

Drásda paused impatiently. 'We don't have long,' she snapped at her cousin. 'I cannot recreate that particular Tear again. If we delay any longer, it would destroy everything we have worked for. Come. We are running out of time.'

Maytra looked at the woman and hesitated a scarce moment before nodding and hurrying after her cousin. The more she looked around, the more she realised that something in the realm was wrong. While it was so beautiful and seemed peaceful, the magick in the air told of a deeper story. If only she knew what it meant.

They rushed through the scenic realm, with not a moment to spare to rest and enjoy. They followed a pure white river as it flowed across the flat landscape. In the distance, to their left were several great, rolling hills. As they moved, a gap between the hills became visible, and a pure white city could be seen, nestled safely among them. A towering red citadel overlooked the city, shining brightly in the light. Maytra slowed to stare at its resplendent beauty.

'But ... this is impossible. It just cannot be...' she murmured, her eyes wide.

'No time!' Drásda said as she grabbed Maytra's wrist, dragging her along behind her. 'You'll understand soon enough.'

But Maytra could not help but stare at the distant place, her cousin the only one keeping her moving. She felt somewhat disheartened as the view was slowly blocked again by the hills, once again hiding the city from sight.

How can this be? she asked herself. *Why is this all so familiar? This place? This feeling?*

The winds.
The winds of magick.
I can feel them.

The passing of Time.
With every moment an age passes me by.
What Time will I come?

What else has changed?

Chapter 17

Clarity and Confusion

Qyesar listened carefully to the Gathering, using it as a way to distract from Lee's obvious change in appearance. The matters the Vertex discussed were pertinent only to their race for the time being, but he found it vaguely interesting. Besides, it took a lot of his concentration to understand their tongue, sufficiently holding his attention. It was a rough language, but it hissed and whispered throughout the hall, as though the words were also shadows. The sounds were darkly beautiful in nature, provoking his imagination to create images of shadow.

The words returned to their nonsensical mutterings as he glanced at his charge. Lee sat straight up against him, his face still changing. Once again, it distracted him from the discussion, and he found it hard to listen again and make sense of it.

What bothered him most was the boy's apparent obliviousness to his changing self. Either he had no idea, or the changes just did not bother him, as though he had expected it or accepted it. Or perhaps, both. The golden eye and streak in his hair had just been the beginning. From the moment he had shown them that vision, other changes had begun, slow and unnoticeable until the change became apparent. It was as though the vision had changed the boy. Changed him into something else.

The most prominent changes were on the left side, as though they were the stronger changes. The right, however, was slowly starting to show different changes as well. His left eye had become golden in colour, glittering brightly even in the shadowed room. His hair had grown out to shoulder length, the left half blonde, turning white, while the right was slowly becoming blue-black. His right eye had growing streaks of black in it.

Another change was his age. He was no longer a young boy, but looked to be between twenty and twenty-five. The change disturbed Qyesar. It was unnatural and the effect was almost scary.

Lee frowned slightly at Qyesar, not liking the intense stare that he was receiving. He felt unfairly scrutinised and he could see judgement in the man's eyes. He had not chosen this, but it was his destiny.

'What are you staring at?' he asked, his voice hushed so as not to disturb the meeting.

Qyesar turned his gaze back to the Leaders. 'Nothing,' he replied, the lie ringing through his voice.

'What's bothering you, Qyesar. Is something wrong?' Lee persisted, wanting the man to tell him outright, rather than just stare.

Before he could respond, Qyesar heard his name called by one of the Clan Leaders. Vexon stood, pulling the Catréan up with him.

'Quickly. We cannot afford to tarry. The Gatherings move quickly to use the minimal amount of time. We have duties to get back to,' he hissed in Qyesar's ear.

Qyesar nodded, relieved for any reason to get him away from Lee's questions, even if it was for a short time. He followed the Vertex's quick steps to the platform.

The Leader who had called him forth extended a hand. 'Step up and join us, Qyesar Storî, ambassador for the Letrans.'

Qyesar hesitated barely a moment before taking the man's hand. Instantly, he felt a rush of dark power. These men held all the power of the Vertex combined and it swept over him, filling him for an instant with the shadows from which they were made.

Pushing the sensation aside, he stepped up onto the platform, unsure of what was to come. He felt somewhat self-conscious, every gaze in the room on him. He had never enjoyed being the centre of attention.

The Leader smiled and embraced him in a clear sign of friendship and acceptance. Once released, Qyesar found himself being similarly embraced by each of the Leaders in turn, each filling him with different aspects of their power. The first of the Leaders turned from him to address the Gathering.

'Vertex!' he called, his voice echoing loudly around the room. 'You now gaze upon our newest ally, the ambassador for the Letrans with whom we side. Éscaronôvic will always remain present in our memories and he did much for our people.

'While none of you yet know this man, it is your task and ours to welcome him and teach him our ways. While you may find it hard to trust him, he is the one named by Scarien, and his judgement we *do* trust. Even in death, Éscaronôvic knew what he was doing. He always did. We must now assume that he was doing the right thing when he broke his Oath.

'Storî is the one we will now turn to. He alone from the worlds above will directly influence our actions, with advice from his leader and from his own judgement. We will come to trust him as he holds his position. Only time will tell if he is truly the right person for his task.

'He will be, the next few months, here, with his charge, to learn of our customs and beliefs. As many of you may remember, Scarien found them hard to understand at first, and therefore, we must allow this man the same courtesy and time to understand our race and to follow in our traditions for as long as he is among us.'

He then turned to Qyesar and nodded, 'The Vertex are with you. Here, you will always have a safe place to stay and rest. If you are ever in need of help, call and we will come to your aid. Now, return.'

Glad to have been dismissed, the Letran officer stepped down from the platform and followed Vexon back up to their seats. He could still feel the stares of the Shadowmen and it sent a cold chill up his spine.

Note to readers:

I am sure you have all experienced that strange and almost bizarre sensation of being watched, or shivering for no particular reason. The strangest of explanations have taken us from the truth of the matter. It is not someone stepping over the site where your grave will be. After all, what if you were examining a volcano and it erupts in your face. I highly doubt someone would be walking over your grave then. A close explanation is the presence of a ghost, although ghosts cannot appear anywhere; they can only be found at the site of their death as long as their body is nearby. Most spirits do not even desire to take a form.

No. Those shivers and sensations are caused by the watchful gaze of the Vertex. Their hidden, ghost-like presence in the shadows can be detected by most. Their intense gaze is infused with an uncharted power.

Do not be fooled, however. The Vertex observe all, not one person being of any special importance to them, save the Children of Destiny. *They watch to better understand the changing realms above them.*

Either that, or you're just completely paranoid.

To resume:

He glanced at the clearly still-changing boy and murmured a soft question to Vexon. All eyes turned to him as though everyone had heard. The Vertex before him just shook his head and put a finger to his lips, shaking his head.

Qyesar nodded, looking around uncomfortably. He was clearly not permitted to speak during Gathering except to contribute. Or maybe it was the topic under which he asked. Maybe it was not to be spoken of. Either way, he nodded and remained silent as he slipped into his seat, deep in thought and with every intention to ask questions later.

Unseen to his guardian, Lee grinned, a dark shadow crossing his face for an instant. He wondered how long it would take for the man to figure out what he now was. For indeed, he was something new.

So much resists me.
They all do.
But nothing matters.

All I need…

…is to succeed.

Chapter 18

Ally

Mattias did not hesitate to react. He flung a fireball in the direction of the sound, watching it light up the passage before disappearing into darkness. Something hissed, and the faint outline of a figure could be seen in the dark.

The group edged backwards as one, moving closer to their destination. Tæmî was shaking with fear, her eyes wide. None of them could tell what their follower was, or what it wanted. Their guesses did little to encourage them, however. The fear created by a follower was amplified by their surroundings.

Mattias lit another fireball, holding it high. *~Caya, can you light up the passage with another one of your were-lights? We might be able to see what it is,~* he said telepathically, not wanting to break the silence.

Caya nodded, even though she knew he was not looking her way to see it. A bright light appeared soon after, enclosed in her hands. As she released it, it floated up above their heads to join the one already hovering. With only a thought for instruction, the light smoothly moved back up the passage to the source of the sound, stopping instantly above a strange creature.

It immediately cringed away from the light, trying to find darkness again. The light, however followed. 'Please,' it hissed with a strange voice, 'It hurts. It hurts us all.'

Caya dimmed the light without hesitation, feeling sorry for the creature and shocked at its pain. The light moved slight away from it as well, giving it a little darkness to cower in.

The creature kept its distance, watching the five people carefully. It seemed confused, lost. 'Where are we?' it asked slowly.

Camer stepped forward slightly to get a better look at it. It had four spider-like arms and huge golden eyes which took up much of its face. Its whole body was thin and spidery and it glistened silver in the dim light.

Suddenly, its eyes flashed red, a new voice speaking, filled with desperation. 'Help us get home. They stole us from there.'

Deep blue eyes accompanied the next voice. 'They would kill us. They brought us here. This strange place.'

Darkness

The creature kept pleading, its different voices desperate, some even child-like, all with a hiss in them.

Camer stopped listening after a few minutes, piecing together what the creature knew of its own story. His eyes glowed slightly green as he spoke to it. 'Raamé. Silence,' he ordered, seeming much taller than his actual height. 'Your home is far. What brings you to Cyphia?'

The Raamé stepped forward, silent for once. It sniffed the air, perplexed. 'You know us? How?'

'As the first Guardian, I know what I must. You are a creature of my element. Why do you not return to Nastraamé? Why linger here?'

The being gazed at him in awe, a swirling mass of colour filling its eyes. 'Foretold one, you have come. You will save Nastraamé. You will save us all.'

'Answer the question!' Camer snapped. *~The Raamé are unable to cause harm. We need not fear him,~* he added to the rest of the group.

'We were stolen. Sucked through. We could not escape the *kexarto.*'

~What is kexarto?~ Scortia asked, confused.

~If there were a translation for it, that is what we would hear. What do you think Camer?~ Caya muttered.

Camer ignored the girls. 'Where? What caused this?'

'We will show,' the golden-eyed personality said softly. 'First, you must retrieve your prophecy. Others are moving for it as we speak. They follow your lead, Empress. Hurry. We follow?'

Camer nodded distractedly. 'Yes. You follow,' he muttered before looking directly at the Raamé. 'Follow us and protect. No one is to follow us. No one.' He turned to the others. 'Let's go. We don't have time to waste.'

~Are you just going to trust that ... thing?~ Scortia asked incredulously, looking at the Raamé with the same stare as she gave bugs.

~Do you not trust me?~

~You've changed, Camer. And remember, you were not quite trustworthy before?~ Mattias murmured.

~I remember, but this is different.~

'Stop bickering, all of you. He's right. The Raamé can always be trusted. Their word is their bond and it is impossible for them to cause harm either directly or knowingly indirectly. They cannot cause or be violent deliberately, and they are near impossible to manipulate,' Tæmî exclaimed, getting frustrated. 'Let us hurry and be gone from this place.'

With their newest acquaintance in tow, the group hurried off down the tunnel, the lights following above their heads. The Raamé's eyes had settled on a deep red

Darkness

and it seemed more tolerant of the light now that it had had time to acclimatise to it.

It was not long before they heard voices rapidly approaching from behind them. They were faint and far off for the time being, but they could tell that their followers were moving faster than they were.

'They have only just entered the tunnels. Keep moving,' Tæmî murmured softly. 'They cannot catch up with us *that* fast.'

Scortia murmured under her breath, a slight breeze picking up and blowing down the tunnel towards them. The words of the guards were carried on the wind to their ears.

'What was the Empress thinking, trusting those strangers? They may have been children, but you can never be too sure. Especially as they have that sort of power,' one guard muttered to his companions.

'Maybe too powerful to subdue. We may be unable to rescue the Empress.'

'We have to. Regardless. We are sworn to protect her till death take us. To give our lives for her,' a third man scolded.

The mutterings continued, nothing good to be said about the *Children of Destiny*. The group listened as they moved onwards, the tunnel starting to slope upwards.

'What?' they heard a guard shout incredulously.

'I'm telling you, we've been here before. We're going around in circles!'

'That's impossible. We've been following the Empress's trail. And once in this tunnel, it's straight.'

The children stopped, looking at each other in confusion. Glancing around, they noticed that the Raamé was missing from the group.

Tæmî looked equally confused. 'As long as they are following me, they cannot get lost down here. It is literally impossible to circle back on yourself once this far,' she whispered.

The Raamé appeared suddenly next to them, its red eyes seeming positively gleeful. They all wondered when it had slipped away, but were, in part, glad to see it again.

'They cannot follow. The Foretold one said none to follow.'

The group laughed lightly in relief, finally free of followers.

Caya turned to the Raamé, slightly concerned. 'Can they get out, though?'

'Of course they can, if they turn back. We never harm. We cannot harm. All we did was stop following.' It

Darkness

gestured on ahead, ushering them forwards. 'Hurry. It cannot last forever.'

Mattias nodded and took the lead once more, following the sloping tunnel. They could see no end nor corners up ahead. The whole tunnel just seemed to extend on forever. A groan passed through the children with a sense of apprehension. They seemed to be in for a long walk ahead.

At least, that was what it seemed to the group. Tæmî, however, baffled them by stopping shortly after they had lost their followers.

'This way,' she smiled, stepping into the mass of writhing insects that cloaked the wall. She vanished from view, leaving the others alone.

Camer was the first to react, stepping through quickly after her. He had examined the area the moment she disappeared and had found very subtle differences in the stone.

Mattias frowned and looked at his sisters. *~Am I missing something or did they just walk into a wall?~*

'We must follow them,' noted the Raamé before following its two predecessors.

Scortia shook her head frantically, keeping as much distance as possible between herself and the walls on both sides, trying to stay away from the creepy-crawlies. *~No* *way. Not me. Never.~*

Caya sighed in annoyance. *~Come on, Scortia. They are just a few bugs. We'll be dealing with worse in the future,~* she coaxed gently, looking at Mattias as she spoke.

The girl shook her head emphatically. *~I'm not going any closer to them!~*

Mattias rolled his eyes. *~Yes you are. We don't have time for this and you can stop being so stupid,~* he muttered, pushing her into the wall.

Taken by surprise, Scortia had no chance to stop herself before passing through the bugs and wall. The section was apparently an illusion and she fell into the room beyond. As she passed through the sea of non-existent creatures, she screamed, her eyes screwed shut. She tried to shut out all thoughts of the bugs, but they filled her mind. All she could see were the monstrous insects, and as she hit the ground on the other side, she curled up into a ball, blocking out everything.

Back in the passage, Caya just glared furiously at Mattias.

~What?~ he asked, shrugging as though he had done nothing wrong. *~She had to go through. I got her there.~*

Caya just shook her head, muttering as she stepped through the wall herself, *~There are other ways. Better ways.~*

She looked around at the room they were now in.

Darkness

There were no bugs here and the walls were clear, shimmering with all kinds of iridescent colours.

Camer was gently shaking Scortia. ~*Come on, you're okay. The insects are gone.*~ The boy looked completely out of depth, his eyes temporarily regaining a child-like quality.

Caya shook her head yet again and crouched down to take over. She rolled her sister over, taking a more effective method; she slapped her hard.

'Scortia Redings, get a grip!' she said firmly and loudly, emphasising every syllable.

Scortia shot back to reality in an instant, her face stinging. A bright red handprint marked her face where she had been slapped. She sat up, looking around carefully, suddenly feeling very weak and stupid in front of the others.

Mattias stepped through a moment later, looking back at the place he came through. ~*That was weird,*~ he commented.

Scortia pushed him back through the wall angrily with a sharp blast of air. As the dazed Fire Wielder returned, she hit him again, forcing him once again back through the wall.

'Stop!' Caya insisted, preventing Scortia's third

attack.

Mattias hesitantly stepped through again, prepared to dodge. However, Scortia just turned away and looked around the room. She frowned, chewing her lip slightly.

'It's just a big, empty room...' she said, her words directed at Tæmî. She turned her gaze to the Empress. 'Is this a joke?'

Tæmî shook her head. 'You're just not looking properly.'

The children exchanged a glance, Mattias's antics apparently temporarily forgotten. None of them could see anything but an empty room.

The Raamé appeared to frown, its features somewhat contorting. 'What is that?' it hissed, its question also directed at the Empress. It pointed towards the centre of the room.

Tæmî followed its finger, clearly confused herself now. 'What is what?' she asked. 'Nothing has ever stood there.'

'The light. The great column of light.' It stepped towards the spot, curious. It was the only one to see this light, and wanted to know what it was.

Camer frowned, his eyes glowing a dim green once more. 'Stop,' he muttered. 'Stop. Do not touch it.' He looked around at the rest of the room as more came into his sight. 'Where is everyone?' he asked.

'They will come when the time is right,' Tæmî murmured.

'But we don't have time to spare. There are people waiting on us. We're needed elsewhere already,' Scortia exclaimed. 'We cannot wait!'

'You can and you must. Trust me on this. It doesn't matter how long you wait, you will leave here at the right time. You needn't worry about that,' Tæmî replied.

Nevertheless, the children could not help but wonder if the Empress was telling them the truth.

The Oracles.

They will know the answers.

So many questions.

But how to ask?

I do not exist.

Yet…

Chapter 19

Wrongness in the Shadows

Vlökir sighed nervously, looking around him as he walked. The Gathering had been more enlightening than he could ever have anticipated. So many different events were being tied together by outside knowledge, but everything seemed to be presented in riddles. There could be no coincidences. Not anymore. But he felt like it was up to him to make sense of everything, to see the bigger picture.

He wandered aimlessly throughout Vantrörkî with Sarýya. The woman had taken it upon herself to watch over the boy while his father was still recovering. He was glad for her company; she reminded him somewhat of his mother.

Passing through the shadows of many different

realms, he puzzled over what he had seen and heard over the last few hours. He had picked up on more than most, noticing even the subtlest of things said and shown. Something seemed wrong with the Gathering. As well as what had been said, there was much that had not been spoken of. To Vlökir, it was this that seemed most important. If only he could make sense of it all.

'What did that vision mean?' he asked Sarýya. 'What was it that wasn't said?' He had only been able to discern that the black egg was wrong. He could feel that it was wrong, but he needed to know why. Maybe one of the Great Ones to come again. Other than that, he had been puzzling over it for over a week.

'The realms are changing. Everything we know, and have ever known, will change,' she replied anxiously, having been on edge since the Gathering. 'Death rides the wind and will come ever more swiftly if you cannot find the answers,' she added, a glazed look in her eyes. The words did not sound as though they came from here, but that instead, she was the vessel through which they were spoken.

Vlökir set about understanding what she had said with even less success than interpreting the vision. It was a riddle, no doubt about that, but the solution eluded him.

Darkness

The matter just seemed too foreign to comprehend.

'The answers to what, though?' he asked after a long period of contemplation. 'How can there be an answer if there is no question?'

'Maybe you have to find the question first, Vlökir. Or maybe you will know the question when you find the answer. I am sure you will understand when the time comes,' she replied with a slight sigh.

'But why do you tell me this?'

'I don't know,' she murmured, looking thoughtful. After a moment, her eyes glazed over again, clearly having more to say.

'This message has been passed down through the generations for the ears of the *Children of Destiny*'. Do not question the Balance for it keeps all in line. There is a time and a place for everything. You will know the question when the time requires you to. The answers are up to you. There is more going on than you know, Guardian.'

'But I am not a *Child of Destiny*. The four have been chosen. I know them,' Vlökir said with a frown.

'You know them well and understand their way more than any other. There are more than four. Remember the Great Ones. And then there is the Balance.'

'If what you say is true, what am I Guardian of?'

'You must discover that yourself, Child of Darkness. Your time will come. Ask the right questions. Nothing is as it seems. The lies must be uncovered. Time must be restored.

'You have already begun. In querying what I have said, you have asked the first correct question. Reflect deeply, for the answer is right before you.'

Vlökir nodded, puzzling silently over what Sarýya had said. Again, he doubted that she was the one speaking, even though the words came from her mouth.

He watched her carefully as she returned to normal, unsure of what had passed between them. She did not seem to recall any of the conversation and smiled gently at him.

'Sorry. What were you saying Vlökir?' she asked.

'Nothing. I think I understand now,' he replied. To be honest, however, his head was spinning from the events that were turning his life upside-down. It seemed as though they were not happening to him, but instead he was looking through the eyes of another.

As he resumed their walk through Vantrörkî, he was thinking hard. If he was indeed a *Child of Destiny*, why was he here? Surely he was needed with the others. Where did he fit into the picture? And who was his opposite?

Pushing thoughts aside, he turned his attention to their location in the realm. Although he was still young, Vlökir knew much of Vantrörkî well. In fact, he was more familiar with the realm than many of his elders, though some areas were still unknown to him. He loved to explore the changeable realm when he had the time to spare. On this particular occasion, he had to stop, looking around carefully. They had come to one of the areas he had not yet investigated.

樂aryýa stopped also, waiting for him to decide where they would go next. She looked up at the wall of the section, old memories surfacing. So much had happened here. She was one of those who had survived the devastating events.

'What's beyond the wall?' Vlökir asked, studying it carefully for any name. The shadows of each realm were permanently walled, the rest of the realm apparently mirroring the Void. There was no indication as to which realm this was.

'Nothing, Vlökir. Not anymore, anyway.'

He turned around to look at his temporary guardian and saw a pang of sadness in her eyes. There was more emotion in her face than a Vertex ever displayed normally.

Frowning, he turned back, wondering what was

different. He tested the wall gently, and then again with more force, but it would not yield. This realm was sealed completely to all outsiders. 'It's shut up tight. What happened here?'

Sarýya sighed. She had come to know the boy well enough to be sure that his questioning would be persistent. He would probably be smart enough to work out what this place had been before on his own.

'The area beyond these walls was once the shadow of Cloric. When a realm falls, its place in Vantrörkî crumbles and collapses. Everyone caught inside was unmade, just as the people of Cloric were killed.'

Vlökir continued to frown, but nodded slowly. 'That would ... make some sense...' he murmured, examining the wall. Something about it did not add up.

Nevertheless, the boy turned away, walking, instead, along the wall, testing it occasionally, but not expecting to find anything different. Finding no weakness he could exploit, he moved away and continued their walk, his mind racing. Something was just not right, but he could not put his finger on it.

As he continued to wander, seemingly aimlessly, he sensed something different. Somewhere nearby was a vast emptiness, as though a whole section of the realm had disintegrated. Such a void could technically never exist in Vantrörkî, and yet he could feel its presence. He glanced toward Sarýya, but she appeared to be oblivious to the sensation.

Looking around, he knew he had followed one of the paths between realms, but he did not know which it was. He was walking to an unfamiliar location with no clue as to what was there to be discovered.

Suddenly, without any warning, the path ended and he was almost thrust into a place of nothing.

Sarýya grabbed him back, her sharp reflexes saving the boy from being unmade. 'Careful,' she warned. 'There is Nothing here, and so nothing can exist here.'

To demonstrate her point, she broke off a clump of shadow from the ground and threw it in the direction of the void. As soon as it reached the line where shadow met nothing, it dissolved, becoming Nothing itself.

Vlökir gazed out over the expanse in a sense of awe. Turning to the shadow around, he grimaced at the sight of great cracks, splintering out from the void.

'This was once the shadow of the realm of the Elementalists, before it collapsed. Nothing was what remained behind. Nothing.'

Vlökir studied what was before him in confusion.

'But ... it makes no sense,' he said. 'Both realms collapsed. So why is there nothing only at one site, when both should be the same?' He looked up at Ŝarýya, his eyes almost gleaming. 'I think something has been missed here.'

The woman shook her head emphatically. 'Not at all. The walls around Cloric sealed up when Vantrörkî began to crack. The walls here should do the same soon enough.'

Shaking his head, Vlökir frowned. 'But it feels different,' he whispered, noting the absence of any wall near the void. How could a wall seal if it was not there? How could a wall exist when it was the walls around the realm that crumbled? And why was there no sense of Nothing behind those walls, if Nothing was what was there?

Studiously examining the area, his senses on high alert, he muttered softly. 'This feels wrong.'

A sign.
A sign of things to come.

The Darkness.
The Nothing.
The Void.
The Light.

They are all connected.
They will release me.

Chapter 20

The Elders

Kaiyén sat motionless, his head in his hands. The situation his people were in grew more dire by the moment. The small ray of hope that remained was slowly dimming. He could only pray that his efforts would soon pay off, that they would see some results. Somehow, however, he knew that would not happen. That it was too late.

He looked up, lifting his head out of his hands, as a woman walked into the room. He gave her a faint smile in greeting, before returning to his previous position. He felt guilt by his action; she always brightened his day and made him smile. However, his weariness and his resignation were taking hold. His hard work all seemed to be in vain, and he could hardly bear to look at her.

Feiyra sighed softly and sat down gracefully next to him. Putting a pale arm around him, she tried to comfort him. 'It's not your fault,' she murmured softly, her voice melodic, reminding him of the way the realm had once been. Her voice could paint so many pictures with the simplest of words; it was one of her major skills. The beauty that the realm once held threatened to bring tears to his eyes.

'Nothing works,' he said in frustration, sounding lost. 'We are cut off from all help and nothing we try can help. There is no magick strong enough. It resists our every attempt. The strain is too great.'

She nodded, thinking quickly, trying to find some way of reassuring him. Picking a flower from the nearest vase, she gently blew over it. The petals curled up and when they unfurled, they formed the wings of a tiny faery, which flew up towards Kaiyén, glittering brightly.

'But maybe it is working. We slowed time to such an extent that maybe we cannot see any effect. By slowing the rate at which it can spread, we may be slowing its destruction. New life can still blossom. You just have to believe in yourself. Then the beauty can return.'

He smiled at the faery, watching it flutter around the room before he looked at her sceptically. 'New life can form, true. We can make it so. And yet, how many have now succumbed?'

Darkness

She bowed her head in defeat. 'Too many. Seventy-eight percent of the population have taken ill and thirty percent of the ill are now deceased.' The faery returned to the flower stem, returning to its former state in response to her disheartenment.

Kaiyén stood and walked across the room. 'So high… We have to find something. Soon. Before any more are lost.'

Feiyra nodded, watching him. 'But at what expense? Maybe we should look outside for help. There must be other solutions. Things we have overlooked. Surely the fourth-realmers…'

'We will not go to those who have already turned their backs on us. They are dead to us,' Kaiyén said, his voice raised almost to the point of shouting.

'But they never turned their backs. They searched for something new and settled for a different way of living. Besides, we cannot blame the descendants for the mistakes of their ancestors. They do not remember ever belonging to our realms. The races of other realms form their mythology, keeping us all alive somewhere in their minds.'

'There will be another way,' he said firmly. He turned to her and sighed, his shoulders slumping as his fury evaporated.

Walking over to her, he hugged her tightly. 'We will save our people. I promise.' He gave her a quick but tender kiss before leaving the room to continue his work.

Feiyra sighed, feeling the sense of containment more than ever. Without the connection to the other realms, their magick was ebbing away. *We need the void. It fuels our realm, that is where the magick is born,* she thought to herself, gazing out of the citadel to the expanses of land beyond. The once bright and colourful landscape was now grey, dead. Only her flowers still bloomed brightly. She sighed sadly, looking around. Even the colour had been lost from the sky.

Our realm is dying. Even if we survive the sickness, how will we survive this?

* * * * * * * * * * * *

Kaiyén made his way down into the main part of the citadel. As he travelled through the maze of rooms, corridors and people, he would stop from time to time to pass on his dwindling energy to those that needed it. He would replenish his reserves with a good sleep. These people, however, would not. That was how the sickness worked. It was like a leech that sucked out the energy from them. And for people of magick, that was a certain death sentence. None ever got better. Only worse until their bodies gave up.

Côrín joined up with him, leaving the spell he had been working on to develop.

'Astiana Kaiyén Almenja,' he murmured as he made a small, but complex, gesture with his left hand. Touching the first two fingers of his right hand to his lips and then his forehead, he murmured, 'The Great Ones have kept you well.'

Kaiyén mimicked the gesture. 'Jenira Côrín Jenréy.' He touched his fingers to his forehead and then to his heart. 'May they keep us both still.'

Côrín glanced around, lowering his voice further. 'Any luck yet? Have you found anything?'

Kaiyén shook his head. 'Nothing works. It mutates faster than we create something to counter it.'

'Is there no way to get ahead of it? Predict its next mutation?'

'We have tried. But it still fails to have any effect. Magick just doesn't do anything.'

Côrín glanced up to the higher part of the citadel, watching Feiyra at the window. 'How is she holding up?' he asked.

Kaiyén followed his gaze. 'She is well enough. She

hates being confined to the upper sections. The number of people she has running around to keep her up-to-date with the news is beyond me.'

'She is just trying to help, Kaiyén. Maybe it's time you let her. Give her a little freedom.'

'I cannot lose her, Côrín. She has to stay out of the reach of this disease. She has to be kept safe. There is too much at stake. She understands that.'

'Very well. That is your decision, but it would not be mine.'

'But you don't understand. None have recovered. Everyone, so far, has died, painfully. I do not wish such a fate on her.'

'What about you, Kaiyén? You know the chances of falling ill. Would you wish her a widow?'

'You know the answer to that.'

The pair walked on in silence, passing their strength onto those they passed. Between them, they had enough hope for all their people, but if hope were enough to save them, time would simply roll back and undo the sickness so that it never would be.

'You and Feiyra...' Côrín began uneasily. The thought had been playing on his mind for many months now. 'You have not...?'

Kaiyén looked at him for a moment before he realised what was being asked. 'Of course not,' he answered. 'Do you not think that we are well aware of what would happen? As Elders, we must never have children.'

Côrín nodded. 'It is not that I do not trust you. I just feared you may have forgotten. Your love for each other seems to blind you both at times.'

'Is it that forgettable?'

'No, not really.'

'Have more faith in me, brother.'

Again, silence fell between them, though Kaiyén could feel the tension between them. He was lying, to his own brother, but he knew Côrín would act as required. His behaviour was predictable, and the occasional reassurance is all he needed. Risking Feiyra was unthinkable. None could ever know about her condition, or the true reason she was kept to the upper levels, isolated from the disease.

The Citadel was great, large enough to keep the entire population between its walls. However, Kaiyén always felt that the journey from top to bottom was never far enough. Conditions felt continually more cramped than reality.

'I think everyone should leave the Citadel,' Kaiyén muttered softly, trying not to raise attention to their conversation. 'The further apart we are, the less this disease can spread. We need to spread out.'

'It's too late to get out now. Have you looked outside lately? On top of that, the piles of dead have risen. None dare go near them to clear the doors. The realm is following in the steps of its people. Cloric has fallen. Can you not feel it?'

'It has not fallen yet, Côrín. There is still time.'

'We cannot hold time forever. It restricts us further from magick, starving the realm. We rely on that element to survive. There is nothing...'

'Shush yourself. Do not speak like that where any can hear. You are right. We cannot hold time forever...' A gleam suddenly entered Kaiyén's eyes. He looked positively overjoyed with his next few words. 'We cannot continue to hold time, but what if we could reverse it?'

'No,' Côrín said firmly. 'No!' he repeated more forcefully as Kaiyén's eyes grew brighter. 'It has never been done.'

'That is not to say it cannot be done,' Kaiyén grinned.

Côrín shook his head. 'This is another one of your mad ideas. If it were anyone other than you spouting this nonsense, I would call it insane, but you already are. I know you far too well. What have you done?'

'Nothing, yet,' Kaiyén murmured, planning out his idea. 'I will see you shortly. Very shortly.'

* * * * * * * * * * * *

Côrín frowned, pacing back and forth. Kaiyén's sudden enthusiasm had worried him somewhat. His brother had hidden himself away for a couple of days now, and there were rumours of something strange happening on the upper levels.

Stopping suddenly, he resolved to go and find his brother before he did something stupid. Knowing Kaiyén, the way that he did, he would end up with some wild magick that threatened his life … again.

As he entered the upper levels, he saw Feiyra sitting at the window. She turned to nod a greeting to him.

'Astiana Côrín. He has been in there all this time.' She pointed towards Kaiyén's study door.

Côrín nodded. 'Thanks,' he said as he strode across the room. Trying the handle, he found the door locked. Typical.

Pressing his ear against the door, he whispered a soft listening spell. From inside the room, however, came silence.

He turned to Feiyra, but she just shrugged, far used to her lifemate's antics. He turned his attention back to the room, listening more intently as the faint hum of magick became apparent.

A loud shout made Côrín jumped, almost out of his skin. Suddenly worried for his brother, he set about forcefully opening the door.

Since forcing the lock proved fruitless, he simply made the door burst inwards towards the wall, ripping off the doorframe in the process. Nothing could have prepared him for what he was about to see.

The first thing he saw was Kaiyén, traces of golden spirals fading from around him. He turned as the door opened and shrugged.

Next to him, was another Kaiyén. This one seemed oblivious to Côrín's presence. He was moving his hands in a strange motion, strands of glittering gold weaving together in the air. After a few seconds, this second Kaiyén vanished.

'Is this not amazing?' Kaiyén exclaimed. 'It works!'

'What are you doing in here, Kaiyén? Have you lost your mind?'

'No, brother. Not at all. Within the confines of this study, I have been able to roll back time for an isolated area, marked by my own boundaries. It really works.'

Côrín nodded to where the other Kaiyén had been. 'What's happened to you? I mean, him.'

'Gone back about five seconds I believe. It was so easy to twist the magick we already use to slow time. By manipulating it, you can keep slowing time until it reverses.'

Feiyra walked over, concerned. 'Kaiyén. What about the consequences?'

He shrugged, seemingly uncaring. 'Nothing needs to change on the outside. Everything can change inside, and as long as the outside remains constant, that seems to have no adverse effects.' He smiled broadly. 'Think about it. Only the Elders need be sent back. That way we can maybe save this realm before everyone falls ill and dies. Change Cloric, but allow all other realms to remain the same.'

Feiyra shook her head gently. 'No. It would not be enough. We must also send out others to find a cure.' She looked between the two. 'What would be better, would be to establish contact with a Cloran on the outside. Ensure that he or she remains hidden from most, but that they find a cure. We can give them the magick they need to get back to when this realm was sealed off. They will need the records of who left, who survived, then we can simulate that again and get the right people out. Minimal interference will be the best method.'

Côrín scoffed. 'I cannot believe I am hearing this. Going back in time is dangerous. What will happen if we change the past?'

'Our realm will prosper. But the outside won't know. The outside will follow the same path as they have all this time since we vanished,' Kaiyén said excitedly. 'We can survive, and then, at whatever time this Cloran is from, we can emerge again, having not changed anything.'

Côrín muttered something in annoyance and looked between the two. Shaking his head he looked directly at Kaiyén. 'What will happen to *this* Cloric. It cannot just vanish.'

'That, I am afraid, I have not thought of yet,' Kaiyén admitted, seeming somewhat sobered at the thought.

'Then, before we do *anything* we need to be sure. Make it perfect. Nothing can change. We will still be sealed off.'

'But maybe not completely,'

Côrín frowned. 'What do you mean? We cannot risk changing anything.'

'I know, but maybe an illusion will be enough to keep them believing.

Epilogue

It is beginning. The visions are spreading, the Balance strained. All that is needed is one more crack. One beautiful crack to release me. To set me free.

The realms cannot last forever. Already I can feel it. It satisfies my hunger, my need, my longing. What is this desire I have burning within me? Burning. Burning.

Darkness will come. Darkness is everything and yet is nothing. Look to the skies and remember the Darkness.

A great black crack through a blood red sky. The magick of the realm is almost visible as it escapes into the Void.

Glorious creation. The spheres will fall. I can feel it now, so clearly. I can hear that sound. The sound that signals my coming.

A great roaring blocks out most other sound. Like the sound of a Gate, but louder. Much louder. Shouts can barely be heard. Children. Shouting. The roar of magick ebbing away.

But it is not enough. Even as it grows to consume, it will not be enough. I need more.

There are children. Standing. Standing near the edge. So near the crack. One stands much further forwards. A girl? It does not matter. She pulls at it. Slows the process.

No! She cannot. She must not prevent it. My destiny has come. She cannot restore the Balance now. It would be wrong to try. Her cries for help fuel my power. She fuels me.

Others shouting, calling her back. She does not listen. She calls to them. Her shouts are loud enough to hear: 'Help me! Help me close it!' The sky swirls, the darkness spreading in vast cracks across the sky. The light dims.

I must stop her. She cannot do this. One realm for my release. That is all I need. One realm. One people. But there is not enough. This realm is wrong. The people are less. Why? The Gates are sealed. Only a Dragon...

THE DRAGONS! How dare they defy me!? I am the one who allowed them to exist. I built this world, this ... existence. They conspire against me. Why? Do they fear me? Once, they all loved me.

Darkness

The Balance, held in a boy. A boy who is no longer a boy. He struggles, trying to keep control. He shows barely an outward sign, however. Maybe it is the fierce concentration in his eyes that betrays him. Or the wavering appearance where the two halves of him meet.

So he is the one. I must defeat him. He holds me back from the realms. The Void, they call it. My playground. My personal toy. I gave them everything. And they forget me. They scorn me. That will all change.

From the void, the spheres can be seen. All realms in existence. Some spheres are cracked, as though they were nothing more than glass. As one shatters, the 'glass' and the fragments of its contents spilling out into the void.

Vantrörkî, shuddering, the Nothing spreading. The realms sustain it. It can be unmade so easily. The Vertex fleeing, with nowhere to go.

Up. Down. Forces of nature. Everything will change. Their worlds will be in chaos. They will fear me this time. They will fuel me.

* * * * * * * * * * *

Up on top of a cliff, the group stood. The blood red sky cracked. Their voices lost in the roaring mix of sound. One stood forward, forcing magick up to the sky. She was slowing the crack from its rapid growth. She was saving them. But she was losing strength fast.

She cried to the others for help, but no help came. They would not, could not. She was alone while they watched. They called her back, but she could not lose a realm. Not now. Not after everything. They had to succeed.

Looking up at the crack she could see into the Void. The vastness of it filled her, frightened her. It was sapping away at her attempts, taking the magick for itself. Chaos would rule.

Suddenly, she felt another fuelling her, providing the extra strength she needed. But it would not be enough. It could never be enough. She blocked the stream. She could not stop now. Scared, she had to continue. She was taken in. They had been right. None of them were ready. She would fail, and it would cost her her life.

* * * * * * * * * * *

The Balance opened his eyes. Both were now golden.

Darkness

Everything he had fought for had been lost. There was no turning back now. He had been released. He could see what happened. The life-force of a child, and not just any child; a *Child of Destiny*. That was what was needed. That energy was what had released him. There was no hope now. He could only hope to fuel the small piece of darkness that remained. The streak of black-blue in his bright white hair.

* * * * * * * * * * * *

Every realm felt it. A vast presence was born. Death rode the winds. Death was coming. And for one girl, Death had come.

* * * * * * * * * * * *

A boy ran forward to the cliff edge, breaking free of his companions. They had not helped her. They had failed. The realm would now fall. He scooped up a chain from the ground. The pendant was unscathed. There was no body. There was no evidence she had ever existed, save for the memories.

The Information and Pronunciation Guide

- Airîn (**Eye**-rin) - Vertex soldier and apprentice Repairer.
- Amerita - Dracona friend of Drásda. Unusually prefers her demorphed form.
- Barek Romà (**Bar**-rek **Row**-mar) - Earth. Belongs to one of the Zyron tournament teams, Qwenox. Very withdrawn and chooses to practice with Iano, never quite involved with the rest of the team, though this may be because of his past. Aged 19.
- Camer Tari (**Came**-er Tar-**ee**) - Earth. Mattias's best friend who supports him. Is chosen to fill a place for the Zynoran. Withholds terrible secrets and is very touchy when asked about his past. Aged 16.
- Catré (**Cart**-ray) - The sixth realm where the *Children of Destiny* have been raised. People = Catréans.
- Caya Éscaronôvic (**Kiy**-a [Kiy rhymes with sky] Esk-**car**-oh-**no**-vik) - Water. One of the *Children of Destiny* who sticks with Scortia throughout. She follows her heart more than her head and cares deeply for any friends she makes. Aged 14.

- Citadel of Tresh - The citadel was the main reason the Clorans were destroyed along with their realm, even though the risks were known, the Clorans still massed together in it.
- Cloric (**Clor**-ick [Clor rhymes with floor]) - The seventh realm and the first known realm to collapse. People = Clorans.
- Clorans (**Clor**-anz) - Invented and discovered all forms of magickal practice and craft, now commonly used amongst the known realms. Thought to be extinct once their realm collapsed but two now continue the line.
- Daesir Muner (Die-**ay**-sear **Moon**-uh) - A new recruit at the Letran camp on Catré. Has a very inquisitive mind. Aged 22.
- Dracör - Zyron tournament team
- Draecik Cerfron (**Dray**-sick **Sir**-fron) - A man in the Letran camp capable of calculating and memorising anything in no more than five seconds. Chairs the mealtime debates. Aged 40.
- Drásda Mîchka (**Draz**-da **Mee**-shka) Lyana's cousin, a Cloran hiding on Drazdéré. She knows more than she will ever say. Created by Sophie Sutherland-Harper.
- Elementalists - The people of the eighth realm - the second to collapse. Their true name and the name of

their realm are hidden to all but themselves.
- Felixi (Feel-**ix**-i) - A group of the Kha'sandric taking the form of an unknown wildcat.
- Francin Birn (**Fran**-sin **Beern**) - Loudmouth recruit of the Letrans who can never keep a secret. Aged 39.
- Ganto Fortoskø (**Gan**-toe For-**toss**-co) - serious high-councillor of the Zyrons. His intentions are never completely clear. Aged 47.
- Haero Furéyin (**High**-row Fure-**ay**-un [Fure rhymes with cure]) - Fire. Belongs to one of the Zyron tournament teams, Qwenox. Youngest team member. He has bright orange hair which he often spikes to resemble flames. He enjoys ignoring Xanor and will often speak his mind when not wanted to. Aged 10.
- Havlerø Samx (Have-**lair**-ro **Samz**) - Khexan – information gatherer.
- Iano Erto (**Yarn**-no **Ert**-a) - Earth. Belongs to one of the Zyron tournament teams, Qwenox. Enjoys sculpting with his powers and often trains solely with Barek. Aged 18.
- Jake - One of the news reporters on Catré. Aged 43.
- Jared Frèska (Jar-**red Fresh**-car) - Water. Open-minded high-councillor of the Zyrons. Enjoys learning of the world beyond Mount Zircon but is very impatient.

Aged 36.
- Jasor Týrn (**Jay**-saw Tire-n) - Soldier for the Letrans. Cooks whilst Mattias is hospitalised. Friendly disposition. Aged 19.
- Jassy Côlot (Jas-**see Call**-lot) - Sergeant of the Zyron army. Aged 32.
- James Greenwood - Possible alias for Jay Fenwood.
- Jay Fenwood - Human liaison for the Letrans, based in the fourth-realm.
- Kanrec (**Can**-rek) - A group of the Kha'sandric taking the form of a wolf.
- Kerianna Mrya (**Keh**-ree-**an**-nah **Mree**-yah) - Letran Inter-Realm Connections Advisor – aware of many different customs and traditions for the known realms and is in charge with most correspondences.
- Kha'sandric (**Kar-sand**-rik) - The collective term for the translucent creatures roaming Mount Zircon.
- Kithara Noyá (Kee-**tar**-a Noi-**a** [Noi as in noise]) - Advisor to the high-councillors of the Zyrons. She plots against all with a thirst for power. She knows right from wrong, yet never seems to distinguish them. Aged 29.
- Lee Redings - Scortia's guardian's son. Has a habit of getting others into trouble. One of the remaining

Clorans though he was not originally aware of this. His predictions are crucial to the Elementalists. Aged 12.

- Letrans (Lay-**trans**) - Group of Elementalists led by Scarien. Oppose Zyrons.
- Lyana Marō (Lee-**aan**-a **Mar**-oh) - Female soldier for the Letrans with a sense of humour and a soft spot for Mattias. Aged 23.
- Mattias Conramesienos (Mat-**ty**-us Con-ra-**mee**-see-**ane**-os [ane as in bane]) - Fire. One of the *Children of Destiny* who currently remains with the Letrans. He hates being the centre of attention and would rather lead a normal life. Aged 15.
- Maytra Redings (**My**-tra) - Scortia's guardian. One of the remaining Clorans though she did not know it at first. Aged 35.
- Nephr Coyra (**Neff**-er Coy-**ra**) - Caya's guardian. Though a free Elementalist, her loyalties lie with the Zyrons. Despite this, she would always support her charge, no matter the decision. Aged 38.
- Nesqo Wirta (**Ness**-ko **Weir**-tah) - Air. Belongs to one of the Zyron tournament teams, Qwenox. Has a habit of levitating wherever and whenever. He has blond hair, which is always cut short and he easily loses himself, and others, in his thoughts. Aged 21.

- Pican Coyra (**Pie**-can) - Caya's guardian. Unaware of his wife's true identity. He is a true Catréan. Aged 38.
- Qwenox (**Kway**-nox) - One of the Zyron tournament teams preparing for the upcoming Elementalist tournaments.
- Qyan Aguana (**Key**-an Ag-**uan**-nah [uan as in iguana]) - Water. Belongs to one of the Zyron tournament teams Qwenox. Always wears black leather with cape. Is very solemn and does not enjoy socialising. His hair is shoulder-length and also black. Aged 15.
- Qyesar Fortern (Key-**ay**-sar For-**turn**) - Soldier for the Letrans. He possesses unnatural strength. Aged 43
- Qyetari (**Kyuh**-tar-ree) - A group of the Kha'sandric taking to the skies
- Sandri (**Sorn**-dree) - One of the news reporters on Catré. Aged 37.
- Scarien Éscaronôvic (**Scar**-ree-in Esk-**car**-oh-**no**-vik) - Leader of the Letrans and the father of the *Children of Destiny*. He is the one who began the divide, causing the realm of the Elementalists to collapse. Aged 39.
- Scortia Éscaronôvic (**Score**-she-a Esk-**car**-oh-**no**-vik) - Air. One of the *Children of Destiny*. Wilful and headstrong. Aged 14.
- Senti Bustra (**Sent**-tee Bus-**trah**) - Air. Warrior for the

Zyrons, remaining enlisted by force. Holds many secrets and would willingly leave the Zyrons when the opportunity arises. However, certain information forces him to remain whether he wishes it or not. Aged 28.

- Tæmî (**Tie**-me) - Empress of Dra'noxia, one of the Circle. Created by Anouska Fox.
- Tasi Chôno (**Tar**-sea **Chore**-no) - Air. Belongs to one of the Zyron tournament teams, Qwenox. Cannot compete for she has come of age and is therefore too old for child tournaments. Aged 25.
- Thenqo (**Ten**-ko) - A formless group of the Kha'sandric.
- Tresh - Capital of Cloric. Its citadel was the reason for the fall of the Clorans.
- Triska (**Tris**-ka) - One of the news reporters on Catré.
- Vantrörkî (Van-**trur**-key) - The shadow realm. This realm is the shadow of all realms, known and unknown, and the Void.
- Vertex (**Ver**-tex) - The people of Vantrörkî. Plural Vertex. Also known as Shadowmen and Sleepbringers.
- Verton (**Ver**-tan) - Camer's guardian Dragon – trainer and protector of the Guardian of Earth.
- Vexon Narønya (**Vex**-on Nar-**own**-nya) - Vertex guide for Qyesar and Lee. High-ranking and possible candidate for future Leader.

The Elementalists Series

- Vyus Samrí (**Vee**-us Sam-**ree**) - Earth. One of the *Children of Destiny*. Murdered at the age of two.
- Xanor Inflárno (**Zane**-or In-**flare**-no) - Fire. Belongs to one of the Zyron tournament teams, Qwenox. Enjoys taking control, even when it is not his place. Has red hair which hangs mop-like over his head. Aged 17.
- Xanja Hôder (**Zan**-ya Oh-**der**) - Vertex officer. Wrote the Destiny Records. Created by Lisa Chacko.
- Xáre - Zyron tournament team.
- Xern - Vertex soldier infused with the Deathscent. Has more control than any other in his condition. Has never killed. Yet.
- Xophîn (**Zo**-fan [fan here is more of a 'fa' with a nasal 'n' on the end, much like how the French say *fin*]) - Vertex guide and father to Vlökir. Helps the children in any time of need.
- Zech - Vertex searcher. Can hear things no other can.
- Zircon - The translucent mountain on Catré which houses one group of Zyrons.
- Zynoran (**Ziy**-nor-an [Ziy rhymes with pie]) - A magickal artefact crafted by the Clorans as gifts for the Elementalists. The Zynoran enhances and focuses the pure elemental power used by the Elementalists in their work. It splits into four to aid a group, brought together

in friendship.
- ➢ Zyrons (**Ziy**-rons) - A group of Elementalists led by the high-councillors. Oppose Letrans.

Acknowledgements

Once again, there are many people I must thank for this novel reaching its final stages.

First and foremost, Thomas J.M. Cook. If it hadn't been for you, my love, *Darkness* may never have seen the light for a few years yet. Thanks to you I got moving and got this monster typed up from my miniscule handwriting. I still haven't worked out what I meant by frigan, or trigan, or higan, or whatever it was … (trigur?). Also, on those days where my wrist gave up and my fingers wouldn't move, your love and comfort kept me going. I may have made my condition worse, but at least I got a novel out of it. Also, it is a great honour that you have taken it upon yourself to design my new range of book covers. They really are brilliant and look much better than mine. You are the graphics man and with you, I am in safe hands.

Secondly, to Georgina Scott. You really are one of my bestest ever friends. You have stuck by me and kept me going. Thanks also for proof-reading for me. Really needed it ^^. And you will become an author yourself. You have more than enough talent. Now finish off your novel and polish it off, give it to me and then publish it. :p

Lisa Chacko. You are not permitted to read this book.

Your incessant nagging may have got it finished but it means that if you are reading this you shall die!!! The Qyetari are flying your way. Jokes. You're a great sister, and I will never say it out loud. Be grateful you get it in writing you evil monster.

To Sootie. You can't read because you're a cat, but who cares. You cuddled up to me at night and got me to switch off and sleep, allowing me to have another day to type. Otherwise there would be even more mistakes in this rag. You are my black wonderfulness and I am glad to have a familiar and writing inspiration in you.

Who to next ... I am determined not to categorise this time, but you may leave me no choice, you endless list of names you...

Well, Mum and Dad, you get a mention here. Definitely. Mum, you took my book into hospital with you (and I was really touched) and you have started reading it. I don't know how far in, but it made me feel great. Dad, you picked it up and I got the highest possible praise relayed through Mum. "It's not bad." I know you love it really and it brings out that hidden child in you. Thanks to you both for giving me more confidence to carry on writing.

To everyone at CCHS (Chelmsford) who have asked

questions and spurred me on. Without your support (intentional or otherwise) I may never have kept going. There are too many of you to name, but I will mention especially S2. While you have migrated to S1, you are all stars. What will CCHS be like without you? I may not be a member of S2, but you're all considered my friends and all deserve a mention here. So... Yolly, Charlie, Liz (my Japanese buddy), Hayley, Rachel, CCC, Holly, Charlotte, Monique, Salome, Louise, Emma and Melissa.

Japanese club also deserves a mention, for stealing my Wednesday lunches and giving me a healthy break from writing.

To all St. John Ambulance Braintree and Bocking Cadets and Adults. Both groups of you have seen me through this book. All I ask is Cadets, get moving and get winning some competitions, and Adults, we need to close the old/young gap a bit more. I still only know a few of your names >> Maybe I shouldn't have said that.

Work. Well... here's a problem. I can't thank McDonald's for giving me hours because they really reduced my writing time. However, I must thank McDonald's for giving me hours because it gave me money to get this book published. Also, to all the people at work. Most of you deserve this one. Those of you I work with and know have been questioning and supportive. To the one of you who said you were proud of me even though you weren't my parent, I won't embarrass you by saying your name, but it was really touching. And to my boss. The world really did become a scary place when you said you enjoyed my book. Thank you ever so much for the comment and thank you so much for providing a stimulating and enjoyable working environment. Most of the time... Saturday lunches can be... maybe not.

To all my old friends who don't fit anywhere else, and all my friends in general. Without you guys, I would never have succeeded in writing this much.

To all my online friends, and those around the world. Chris Best, for being a constant source of support. I am sorry my time has gotten restricted lately due to everything. Hope you are well and wish we could talk more. To David in Australia, for being amazing and supportive and encouraging me to keep track of all the countries this book has reached. To Sarah, for being the first person I didn't know to read my book and email me. I really appreciated it and still have your email.

To the people at Lulu.com, who have made everything smooth and easy and kept things quick.

To all the magick in the world. You have given me

the power to create worlds and have inspired me to create these books. To all the colour in the world. You formed the basis for all my description and painted new worlds in my head.

Finally to the Official Monster Raving Loony Party. You have put some fun back into the world and I salute you. What would the world be without you. You deserve every vote in the country.

Extract from Shattered

If you cannot wait for the next chapter to be available, read on.

Prologue

He looked down the mountainside one more time. As a Hunter, he could leave the confines of the village freely, but he was not free. He could not leave. Not now. Not ever.

He looked at the realm beyond. It was beautiful. He wished to go out to it and escape this place. But he was held back. There were no physical or mental chains, but he was chained nonetheless. There was nothing really stopping him leaving, but everything did.

He shook his head slowly and moved down the mountain, taking the less-travelled paths. He could see some of the other Hunters ahead of him, already well on their way to trade. The Council would never be free of the fact that the village needed supplies. Nothing would grow with the artificial light and animals would not grow or thrive inside the mountain. Something repelled them. The type of magick was wrong for this realm.

The other Hunters suddenly ran for the trees. The farthest reaching stretch was well within their running distance. This was a trading mission. They carried no weapons. These Hunters were fast and light on their feet. In the forest, they would take to the trees. The Felixi were clumsy in the trees.

He looked to the skies. The Qyetari were circling, their

movements consistent with their attack formation. They knew these Hunters, and they were angry.

He jumped down to more open territory, keeping his eyes on the Qyetari, who drew ever closer. They ignored him, still focussed on their prey. As the Hunters dove into the trees, the Kha'sandric crashed into the branches before taking to the skies again. Their eyes burned brightly, silver light, resembling the light of the moon, illuminating the ground below them.

They were getting smarter, there could be no doubt. Could it be that they were regaining part of their old selves back? He could not tell, but he had a duty to protect the Hunters.

Duty. Duty was a funny thing. It defined all his roles and conflicts. He had a duty to stay, and yet a duty to leave. He had a duty to protect both Hunters and Kha'sandric. He had a duty to the village. He had a duty to the realms beyond. The only one he had no duty to, was himself.

He watched the airborne creatures for a few moments longer. Deprived of their hunt, they had begun to move away, most likely to find food. Their numbers were increasing, that much he could tell. In the beginning, there were only five. Five created by the Council. Created, he remembered, to keep him here, even though they had encouraged him to leave and find his own way.

He could still pick out who was who. His mother, father, wife and two children. They were all going to leave once. But they were stopped. The Council would not let a good Hunter leave. They would not let a whole family leave. The mountain needed something to protect the village against all intruders, and so this was what they had created.

They were not just any family. They were his family. It had been so long ago now. Only the oldest of the Council knew of it. He stayed to protect them, for the Kha'sandric were uncontrollable. They did not only attack intruders, they attacked all, thus putting themselves in danger of being slaughtered by the Zyrons, the very people who had once known and loved them as people.

The large flock turned again, fixing on Senti. He spotted them, and remained motionless, watching. If only they would recognise them. If only there was something left of their old selves.

It did not take long for them to turn away once more and disappear around the mountainside. He felt a pang of sadness at seeing them leave, but was glad he had not needed to hurt any of them today. Sure, they would revive in a different form, but he was convinced that the process caused them some pain.

The Qyetari flew high, soaring above the clouds. One of them flew slightly behind the flock, something different about its motion. The Qyetari in question glanced behind it once again just as the man was lost from view. Something was stirring inside them. They were waking up. The more they revived, the weaker the magick became. They would never return to their true forms again, but they could regain themselves.

Senti... *it thought softly, the name whispering around the mountain, soaring on the gentle wind.*

The mountain responded, alive also. Its thoughts were old, deep. Senti, *it murmured back, rumbling softly. It knew this man. He was a good man and respected the mountain.* Senti.

Shattered

Coming 2011

Other books by Hannah S. Chacko

When Scortia runs away from home, new forces begin to move.

She thought her life was tough.

She thought she could no longer cope.

How will she fare in this new world she has entered?

A world to which she always belonged…

…but never knew existed.

And soon her best friend, too, is dragged into this dark and dangerous time.

Secrets are revealed.

Prophecies are born.

But can they survive the Elementalists' war?

The Lie is also coming soon with a new face.

About the Author

Hannah S. Chacko is an 18-year-old A-level student at Chelmsford County High School for Girls. She is studying for her last exams this summer in Biology, Chemistry, Maths and Psychology.

Hannah has been a keen writer since she was six years old and has been a keen reader for much longer. She enjoys writing fantasy, dark fantasy and horror stories for all ages. While currently working on the *Elementalists* series, she has several other books and short stories under construction.

A fond lover of cats and a hater of sports, she can often be found with a notebook or laptop in tow and spends a lot of time with her boyfriend, relaxing and watching CSI, Family Guy and South Park. She supports the OMRLP and wishes there was looniness in the world.

Printed in Great Britain
by Amazon.co.uk, Ltd.,
Marston Gate.